"Kara, lis...

Jake's footfalls pounded behind her. She ran faster. "Kara," he called. "If you didn't set the fire, you have no reason to run," Jake called. "The police will protect you from whoever you're afraid of."

She tripped over the curb as she chanced a glance over her shoulder.

Jake burst from between the houses just as she recovered her balance. His gaze slammed into hers. The dim light couldn't mask the concern she saw flickering in his eyes. "I can help you, Kara."

The sound of a siren broke his spell. He'd called the police. She gulped in a lungful of air. "If you really want to help me, Jake, forget you ever saw me." She turned on her heel and ran.

"Kara!"

Blinding headlights blipped on, and she froze. Her heart jammed in her throat as the lights sped toward her. *I'm going to die.*

Hurled into the hedges on the other side of the road, her body exploded in agony. Then everything went black.

Books by Sandra Orchard

Love Inspired Suspense

*Deep Cover
*Shades of Truth
*Critical Condition
 Fatal Inheritance
 Perilous Waters
 Identity Withheld

*Undercover Cops

SANDRA ORCHARD

hails from the beautiful countryside of Niagara, Ontario, where inspiration abounds for her romantic suspense novels. Not that she runs into any bad guys, but because her imagination is free to run as wild as her Iditarod-wannabe husky. Sandra lives with her real-life hero husband, who happily provides both romantic and suspense inspiration, as long as it doesn't involve poisons and his dinner. But her truest inspiration comes from the Lord, in the beauty of a sunrise over the field and the whisper of a breeze, in the antics of a killdeer determined to safeguard its nest and the faithfulness of the seasons. She enjoys writing stories that both keep the reader guessing and reveal God's love and faithfulness through the lives of her characters.

Sandra loves to hear from readers and can be reached through her website, or at www.facebook.com/sandraorchard or c/o Love Inspired Books, 233 Broadway, Suite 1001, New York, NY 10279.

IDENTITY WITHHELD

SANDRA ORCHARD

⬧ HARLEQUIN® LOVE INSPIRED® SUSPENSE

Recycling programs
for this product may
not exist in your area.

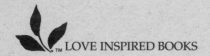

_{TM} LOVE INSPIRED BOOKS

ISBN-13: 978-0-373-67645-3

Identity Withheld

If I rise on the wings of the dawn, if I settle on the
far side of the sea, even there your hand
will guide me, your right hand will hold me fast.
If I say, "Surely the darkness will hide me and the
light become night around me," even the darkness
will not be dark to you; the night will shine
like the day, for darkness is as light to you.
—*Psalms* 139:9–12

To the dedicated volunteer firefighters
faithfully serving our small communities.

Acknowledgments

The Lord's provision when I'm wrestling out a story always
delights and encourages me.

I learn so much and am indebted to the many experts
who tirelessly answer my questions. In particular, I'd
like to thank retired volunteer firefighter Don Gretsinger,
thirty-three-year veteran and retired district chief, Ivan Good,
firefighter Harold Riemersma, and retired fire investigator
Dave MacMullen for answering my many questions.

Thank you to midwife Brianna Timmers for helping me create a
plausible backstory for Tommy's mother. And a huge thank-you
to paramedic Charlotte Cripps for teaching me so much about
emergency procedures, both for this story and Sherri Steele's
story coming next year, and...for connecting me with Dave.

Thank you also to the WODE members who helped me
brainstorm the proposal and work through various scenes.
To Vicki McCollum for her ever-helpful feedback. To my
editors Tina James and Giselle Regus for the many ways they
helped make the story stronger. To Patti Jo Moore for her daily
encouragement and prayer cover. To Nancy Miller for the many,
many little things she does to give me more time to write. To
author Laura Frantz and Amber Perry for answering all my
questions about Seattle and area. To reader Susan Manchester
for telling me about her dog Rusty, the inspiration behind
Tommy's dog. To Kara Grant for loaning my heroine her name.
To the blog readers, newsletter subscribers and Facebook fans
who brainstormed backstory and titles with me, and who made
choosing actors to model my characters after so much fun!

And...a huge thanks to the world's best brainstorming partner,
Stacey Weeks, who put up with countless phone calls and
emails to help me work my way through the smoky haze of
the first draft.

ONE

Jake Steele squinted through the smoky haze surrounding the house, his skin prickling with the sensation of being watched. *There. In the hedges.* It had to be their arsonist. This fire had all the signs of being deliberately set. Jake motioned to his partner, Davis, and they started for the hedge.

The face disappeared, swallowed by the drizzly darkness.

Counting on the suspect wanting to avoid the street, Jake beelined to the backyard. Sure enough, a lone figure skulked along the property's edge. This pyromaniac was going down.

Jake and Davis closed the distance fast, the commotion of the other firefighters masking the thump of their heavy boots. "Where do you think you're going?" Jake grabbed the guy's arm.

The scream that met his grip was no guy's.

Jake turned his flashlight on their culprit, and her panicked brown eyes blindsided him. His grip loosened.

She twisted and squirmed, pounding her free fist against his chest and kicking uselessly at his legs. "Let go of me."

"Fat chance," he said, tightening his grip again. Never mind the tears streaking her sooty cheeks. Men hadn't cornered the market on arson jobs. And with five suspicious fires this side of Seattle in the past nine weeks, he wasn't about to let her out of his sight until he found out exactly what she knew about this one.

She went limp, her fight gone. "You're hurting me."

His gaze shifted to the arm he still held, the *only* part of her he'd touched as he'd let her wear herself out pummeling his chest. His heart pitched. "You're burned." He jerked his thumb off her blistering flesh, sickened that he'd hurt her further.

His partner directed a flashlight at her arm. The underside was flaming red from wrist to crook.

Cupping her elbow with just enough pressure to prevent her from escaping, Jake gentled his tone. "Are you burned anywhere else?"

"I'm fine." She tried to tug free of his hold.

"You're not fine." Megadoses of adrenaline had to be shooting through this spitfire for her to not so much as wince at the pain that had to be blazing up her arm. "This is a serious burn. It needs to be dressed."

She visibly shrank at his insistent tone. "My friend's coming for me. He'll take care of everything."

Right. If she thought he was about to let her walk away, she'd clearly burned a few brain cells along with that arm. Being careful not to cause her any more pain, he steered her toward the street. "You can wait for your friend in the ambulance."

As they came around the now-smoldering building, she dug in her heels and darted terrified glances every which way. "No, please."

Jake caught his partner's attention and jerked his head toward the sheriff's car.

Davis nodded and jogged off.

Jake angled his flashlight just high enough so he could study her heart-shaped face without blinding her. How had he ever mistaken her for a guy? She didn't look much younger than him— late twenties, maybe. Her damp hair, flattened by the rain, skimmed her shoulders, but she was all girl—and very afraid. He'd expected to see fear over getting caught, maybe regret. Not— "I want to help you," he said, his voice cracking at her terror.

Her watery brown eyes searched his as if she

desperately wanted to believe him. "I can't go out there," she whispered.

The rattled pitch of her voice tugged at his heart. He tilted his head, softening his expression. "I'm Captain Jake Steele with the Stalwart Fire Department. What's your name?"

"Ni—" She coughed, the crackly sound rattling through her limbs. "Kara. Kara Grant."

He didn't believe her, but nodded anyway. The cough had all the signs of an attempt to buy enough time to come up with an alias. "Did you set the fire, Kara?"

Her eyes flared. "What? No!" She made another useless attempt to jerk free of his grip as the sheriff and Davis rushed toward them. "Sheriff, this firefighter won't let go of me!"

"She needs medical attention," Jake growled.

"He thinks I set the fire! When I'm the victim here."

"Wait. You live here?" Jake's surprise pitched the question a couple of octaves higher than he'd intended.

"What do you think?" She cradled her wounded arm.

"Lady, you were running away. What do you think I thought?" His department had been called in to assist this neighboring town's volunteer department. He hadn't caught the name of the missing victim. *Her name.*

The sheriff radioed the news to the chief. The firefighters who'd been searching for her inside soon emerged from the house.

Kara gulped. "They were all looking for me? I'm sorry, I didn't realize."

"Didn't realize?" Jake ground his teeth to reel in his tone. "My men were putting their lives at risk while you watched from the bushes. I have a five-year-old boy at home who doesn't need to lose another parent."

"I—" Her expression crumpled. "Please, no one was hurt, were they?"

Jake let out a pent-up breath. "No."

The sheriff cleared his throat. "I still need you to answer a few questions, and I think you'll be more comfortable doing that in the back of the ambulance than a squad car."

Her breathing quickened. "Okay, yes. You're right. Of course."

Since she'd stopped complaining about his hold on her elbow, Jake guided her toward the ambulance. As they stepped into view of her neighbors huddled in their yards, their Thanksgiving dinners forgotten, Kara clung to his coat. Jake scanned the crowd, looking for anyone suspicious. A bulbous-nosed man stood alone and seemed particularly intent on the firefighters' actions.

"It's the tenant," a woman exclaimed.

A young man cut across the yard and raced toward them. At Kara's sharp inhalation, Jake instinctively angled his body to block her from view.

The guy raised something in his hands. A camera.

"It's okay. It's just a reporter," Jake said, shifting back.

But at the camera's flash, Kara buried her face against his coat. "Please, just get me to the ambulance. Please."

His conscience pricked at her sudden trust, or maybe the way she trembled against his chest. He curled a sheltering arm around her. "Sheriff, I think those questions better wait until after the paramedics check her over."

Jake pulled back just enough to see Kara's face. His initial assumptions weren't adding up. He scrutinized her breathing, her eyes, her skin, for signs of assault, shock, something that would explain why she'd run from help.

Besides the obvious—fear of getting caught.

A section of roof crashed to the ground, spewing black smoke and debris into the air and over her car. Kara forced herself to draw deep breaths, to release them slowly. The paramedics were bound to insist on taking her to the hospital, and she couldn't let that happen. Especially now that

Jake's suspicions had confirmed her worst fears. The fire was no accident.

The taste of smoke turned acrid in her mouth. Deep down she'd known the fire was meant for her. That was why she'd called the marshal overseeing her protection the instant she'd gotten out of the house. She shook her head. And then she'd almost let her real name slip to the overprotective firefighter. Thank goodness Mrs. Harboyle had been away at her daughter's for Thanksgiving.

Kara's vision blurred. Her landlady's home was destroyed, along with sixty years of memories, and it was all her fault.

"Hang on," Jake's husky voice whispered through her hair, an instant before his hands spanned her waist and hoisted her onto the back of the ambulance.

Her breath caught. *Oh.* After the way she'd fought him back there, she hadn't expected him to be so nice.

He ditched his hat on the end of the rig, and his sandy brown hair, damp with perspiration, curled over his forehead. "You okay?" he asked, his sweet, lopsided smile not helping her breathe any easier.

Pressing her palm to her chest, she sank onto the gurney. Listen to her. She shouldn't be noticing a guy's smile. Never mind how her heart had twisted when he'd mentioned his motherless son.

No one wanted a relationship with a woman with a price on her head.

Kara startled at the touch of a petite brunette beside her and scrambled to catch up to the questions she was spewing.

"I think she's in shock," Jake said, his deep voice quieting her frayed nerves.

He seemed genuinely concerned. Could he be someone she could trust? Maybe. Except the marshal had warned her not to trust anyone. Not even the police, because a smart bad guy would pretend to be on her side, pretend to want to help her, pretend to be taking her to safety just long enough to get her somewhere secluded and then slit her throat.

She gulped, sliding her hand up to her neck. Stick to the rules, the marshal had said, and she'd be okay. They'd never lost a witness who stuck to the rules.

So how would Deputy Marshal Ray Boyd explain the fire?

She pushed away the female paramedic's stethoscope. "I have to go." For all she knew, the paramedic worked for the adoption ring, too. She glanced from one blocked door to the other, her heart racing. Anyone here could work for it. Be waiting for the chance to finish her off.

"It's going to be okay," the paramedic soothed in the kind of voice Kara used to use with her kindergarten students. "I can quickly dress this wound and then the sheriff can ask his questions. Okay?"

The sheriff, right. Kara wiped sweaty palms down her slacks. She needed to stay calm. If they thought she was in shock, the sheriff might insist she go to the hospital. And it would be way too easy for her attacker to get to her there.

"Kara?" the paramedic's voice filtered through her frenetic thoughts.

"I'm sorry, pardon?"

"I asked on a scale of one to ten, how bad is the pain in your arm?"

"Oh."

Jake stood at the rear door, watching her, his warm blue eyes radiating concern.

She ducked her head. The pain was bad, really bad, but if she admitted that, they'd dope her up and send her to the hospital and she'd miss her meeting. The marshal might not find her.

"Kara?" The paramedic split open what looked like a ketchup packet. "How bad?"

Kara shrugged. "Not bad. Honest. A four maybe."

The paramedic clasped Kara's wrist and started squeezing the packet over the wound.

Blinding pain streaked down her arm. "Ah!" She jerked from the paramedic's grasp. Bandages tumbled to the floor.

The paramedic swiped at the gel that had spilled from the packet onto her leg. "I'd better give you something for the pain," she said through gritted teeth.

Kara thrust out her arm. "No, really. That's not necessary." Nausea churned her gut. She swallowed hard. "I'm sorry. You just surprised me."

The woman raised her eyebrow and slanted a glance at Jake with a slight shake of her head.

Kara tried not to wince as the paramedic dabbed the remaining gel around the blistered portions.

"Most of the burn is first degree," the paramedic explained as she wrapped a bandage around the arm.

Kara swallowed again and again. Why had the marshal suggested a place so far away to meet? With her car covered in debris, not to mention blocked in the driveway by fire engines, she'd have to walk, and…

"These blistered portions are second degree," the paramedic went on. "I'm afraid they're going to hurt a lot more than a *four* before they get better."

Yeah, they already did. A black haze slid over Kara's vision.

"Are you okay?" Jake sounded really concerned.

She teetered, reached out blindly to stop herself from toppling off the gurney.

Jake lunged toward her. "She's going to faint!"

The next thing she knew, her cheek was pressed against his solid chest, his arm wrapped protectively around her. "You're okay. I've got you."

For a few blissful seconds, she lingered in his protective embrace—the kind of embrace Clark should've wrapped her in three months ago.

She sucked in a quick breath and straightened, dismissing the memory. She'd made her choice and so had he. Jake's arm dropped away, and she shivered at the chilly damp air that rushed into its place.

"I'm guessing you'll want those painkillers now?" The paramedic doused the bandage in saline.

The cooling flow took the edge off the pain. "Uh, maybe just a couple of acetaminophen."

Empathy brimmed in Jake's eyes. "You'll have to forgive my cousin. She needs to work on her bedside manner."

Kara chuckled, bringing that heart-fluttering smile back to Jake's lips. She sighed. She would've liked the chance to get to know him. But by tomorrow, Kara Grant would no longer exist.

Another paramedic appeared at the back doors, where the now-missing sheriff had been. "Ready to roll?"

"Roll?" She pushed on the gurney to slide off. "No, I'm fine. I don't need to go to the hospital."

Jake's hands dropped to her shoulders, pinning her in place. "You almost passed out. You're *going* to the hospital."

Kara was about to argue, offer to sign anything they needed to let her leave, then she caught sight of the reporter angling for another photograph and said, "Okay, let's go." If by some miracle the adoption ring wasn't behind tonight's fire, her picture in the paper would seal her fate. A haircut, dye job and colored contacts may have transformed her from a long-haired, blue-eyed blonde, but there was no disguising her heart-shaped face.

One good thing Kara learned en route to the hospital was that the coffee shop where she was supposed to meet her handler was only two blocks away. All she had to do was convince the doctor she was fine and get out before anyone tried to stick her with anything.

Except the triage nurse didn't hold out much hope that she'd see a doctor anytime soon. "The fog caused a huge traffic pileup," she said. "Every E.R. bed is full, and I'm afraid it may be some time before we can even transfer care from the EMT. We need to give priority to the most critical patients."

"Yes, I understand," Kara said, fishing for an out. "Perhaps I should just wait to see my own doctor tomorrow."

"I don't think that's wise," the paramedic— Sherri, she'd said her name was—piped up. "You have no home to go to. And besides, the sheriff is coming here to interview you."

"Okay, then." The nurse recorded all Kara's pertinent details, and then directed Sherri to wheel her into the hall to wait until her care could be transferred.

Not good. She could be stuck for hours waiting for a bed, never mind waiting to see the E.R. doc. "You really don't have to stay with me," Kara said to Sherri after her partner wandered off to do paperwork and restock their rig. "You must have other calls to get to."

"No, not until the hospital takes over your care. That's the policy."

Kara sat up. "If you just need the gurney back, I can sit in the waiting room." She felt silly lying on the thing anyway.

"That's not how it works."

"Oh."

Sherri hitched her hip onto the edge of the gurney. "So how long have you known my cousin?"

"Your cousin?"

"Jake."

"Oh, the firefighter." Kara vaguely remembered him referring to Sherri as his cousin, although they shared little family resemblance. "Just since tonight."

Sherri's head jerked back as if she didn't believe her. "Really? He didn't act like it."

Jake's "It's okay. I got you" replayed in Kara's mind as she realized for the first time that he'd caught her, when Sherri had been closer, right at her side, even.

Sherri studied her intently, her expression unconvinced.

"Why don't you grab yourself a coffee?" Kara suggested.

"I'm fine." Sherri asked her about her family and job and Kara did her best to avoid giving direct answers.

Once more, Kara suggested Sherri get herself a coffee or bite to eat or a breath of fresh air, anything to get her away for a few minutes so Kara could slip out of the hospital. She needed to go before the bad guys figured out she was here. But the woman wouldn't budge.

Kara readjusted her position on the uncomfortable gurney for the umpteenth time in two hours. "What happened to the sheriff? I thought he wanted to ask me questions."

"I'm sure he'll be here soon. Why don't you try to get some rest?"

No, she couldn't do that. It seemed as if every person who walked by looked at her oddly. Any one of them could be a goon of the adoption ring waiting for the chance to finish her off. She needed to get out of here. Somehow she needed to get word to the marshal, but with Sherri hovering so close, Kara hadn't dared even to try to text him. "Um, Sherri? I need to use the washroom." Why hadn't she thought of that sooner?

Sherri smiled, her eyes crinkling as if she genuinely cared, so different from her all-business attitude back in the ambulance. "No problem. I can walk you there." She led her to a single-stall facility.

"Uh, maybe you could find out how much longer the wait will be while I go."

Sherri propped a shoulder against the hall wall. "I'm sure it won't be much longer."

Great, sneaking away is out. Kara shut the door and opted for plan B. She turned on the faucet and the fan and prayed the noise would muffle her voice as she dialed Ray's number. Voice mail picked up on the fifth ring. What did she do now? It wasn't like him not to answer.

A knock sounded on the door. "You okay?" Sherri called.

"Yes. Almost done." Kara lifted her voice over the noise of the fan, and then cupped her hand around her mouth at the receiver. "Ray, it's Kara. They made me come to the hospital and the sheriff wants to question me and… Please come get me if you can. Or I'll meet you as soon as I'm released."

Sherri knocked again. "They have a bed for you. You ready?"

Kara stuffed the phone back into her pocket, snapped off the faucet and fan, and jerked open the door. "Ready."

Rather than return her to the gurney, Sherri led her to a curtained-off bed at the end of a long room lined with beds. "Here you go. Lie down here and the doctor will be in to see you soon." Sherri nodded at the sheriff waiting by the bed, then left. Facing the sheriff alone, Kara suddenly felt a whole lot worse than she had a minute ago.

A very efficient nurse wasted no time checking her vitals as the sheriff pulled up a chair and flipped open his notebook. Between his crisply ironed shirt, unflattering crew cut and the hard lines creasing his face, he reminded her of a drill-sergeant principal she'd once worked under—the kind of guy who didn't let anything slip by him.

"Your pulse is very rapid," the nurse scolded.

Yours would be, too, if someone was trying to kill you! Kara took a deep breath and willed it to slow.

"Tell me what happened," the sheriff said.

"I was upstairs watching a movie in my room when my landlady's cat started scratching my door and mewing frantically." Kara dug her fingers into the sheets. Had she cost Mrs. Harboyle her dear companion, too? "Did the firefighters save the cat? It ran when I tried to pick it up."

With a suppressed huff, the sheriff stopped writing. "A large, long-haired white cat?"

"Yes!"

"Yes, he was rescued. Please continue."

"I turned off the TV and—" She squeezed her eyes shut as the panic crashed over her all over again. "That's when—" Her breath came in short gasps. "I heard the crackling, smelled the smoke."

The nurse touched Kara's shoulder. "You're okay now. Take deep breaths."

Inhaling, Kara pressed her lips together.

"Did you hear anything downstairs before that?" the sheriff asked.

"It's an old house. It creaks and groans a lot. I try not to pay too much attention." She bit her lip. It wasn't a lie, exactly. She did *try* not to pay attention, but with a death threat hanging over her head, every creak and groan made her jump. That was why she'd turned on the movie, extraloud, to drown out the noises of the storm outside, and the one inside her head and heart. She was spending Thanksgiving alone, and couldn't help wondering if she'd ever be able to spend another holiday with her family, as paltry as their celebrations had always been.

"How about outside? A bark? A car engine? Any kind of movement?"

She twisted her hands in the sheets and buried them in her lap. "No, nothing."

"Were you home alone all day?"

"No, I work for a janitorial service." The furthest thing from a kindergarten teacher the marshal's office could find. And she missed being with kids so much. "I got home just after five."

"Was the door locked?"

"Yes."

"And you didn't smell any smoke at that time?"

"No, I reheated leftovers and went to my room."

"You didn't check the other doors?"

"I did." She gulped. She was always checking and double-checking the locks, because Mrs. Harboyle had a bad habit of letting out the cat and not relocking the door.

"And you didn't hear anyone break in? See any evidence of a break-in?"

"No." Kara's throat constricted at the possibility that Mrs. Harboyle had left the back door unlocked before her daughter picked her up. That the arsonist might've still been in the house when she got home.

The sheriff flipped over a page in his notebook. "How did you get out?"

She fixed her gaze on the sheriff's badge. "I covered myself with a wet towel and tried to get downstairs, but—" The words clogged in her throat. The flames had moved so fast.

"That's how you burned your arm?"

She hugged it to her belly and nodded. "I ran back to my room and jumped out the window onto the roof of the woodshed and from there to the ground."

"Did you see anyone then?"

"A car stopped on the street and I hid in the bushes." Her heart ratcheted in her chest at the memory—the fear that she'd escaped the fire only to face the man who'd set it.

"Our 9-1-1 caller. Yes, I talked to him. He said he pounded on the door. Why didn't you show yourself? Tell him no one else was inside?"

"I—" She gulped. "I guess I was in shock."

The sheriff drilled her with the same questions, phrased a dozen different ways, for what seemed like forever. Finally the nurse shooed him out to make way for the doctor. To Kara's relief, he said he had all the information he needed for the moment.

By tomorrow, she'd be out of town and it would be the marshal's problem to explain her disappearance.

The nurse returned with a tall, dark-haired doctor who immediately started into his own litany of questions as the nurse removed the arm dressing so he could examine the burn.

The more questions he asked, the edgier Kara

grew, but she couldn't figure out why. There was nothing weird about his questions. Except...

He never actually looked her in the eye. Not once. Was he afraid she'd be able to read something there?

She muffled a gasp. What if the adoption ring was connected to organized crime and they had a hold over him, like that doctor on the TV show, and they'd ordered him to kill her?

She swallowed. Okay, get a grip. He could just be preoccupied. He wore a wedding band. Maybe he'd just got off the phone with his wife about a problem at home. He had to at least be a doctor, right? Otherwise the nurse wouldn't have brought him in.

The doctor glanced at her now-bare wound. "That doesn't look too bad."

And it didn't. Aside from a few blistery spots, she'd had sunburns that were worse.

"You can go," the doctor said, turning to leave.

"I can?"

Someone stepped around the curtain on her other side, and she practically springboarded into the air.

The person glanced at her in confusion. "Sorry, wrong bed."

Meanwhile the nurse hurried after the departing doctor. "Are you sure? Her BP is low.

And look at her eyes. I'm concerned she's still in shock."

Kara blinked. What was wrong with her eyes? Aside from her overreaction to Mr. Wrong Bed.

The doctor stopped, and for the first time met her eyes, for all of a fleeting nanosecond. "She's fine."

Kara swung her legs off the bed, not about to wait around long enough for the nurse to change his mind. Maybe it was her imagination, but the woman seemed a little too anxious to keep her here.

As Kara pushed aside the curtain to leave, the nurse trotted up carrying a hypodermic. "Hold on a second."

"What—what's that for? The doctor said I can go."

"Yes, but he just ordered this to help with the pain."

"I don't need it." Kara edged sideways, putting the bed between her and the needle-happy nurse. How had she not clued in to that maniacal glint in her eyes sooner? It was the exact same glint she'd seen in that goon's eyes back in Boston when he'd spotted her snapping his picture and pulled his gun.

An orderly popped a wheelie with a wheelchair at the end of her bed. "You the one who's getting sprung?"

"That's me!" Kara jumped into the wheelchair.

The orderly didn't get three feet before the nurse rounded the bed with the needle. "She's not going yet."

"Yes, actually, I am," Kara insisted, reaching for the wheels herself. "The doctor released me."

The orderly hesitated.

"Let's go," Kara prodded, cranking the chair out of the nurse's reach.

"Fine, take her," the nurse relented, and the orderly snapped into action.

"Your ride waiting outside the E.R.?" he asked, wheeling her past the long row of beds and into the hall.

"Uh, no ride."

He pulled the chair into an abrupt U-turn.

"What are you doing?"

"Taking you to the front doors. There's a cab company across the street."

As they passed the E.R.'s reception desk, she glimpsed the nurse talking on the phone and eyeballing her. What if she'd alerted a cohort to cut her off out front?

Spotting an exit sign at the end of the next side hall, Kara said, "Stop, I'll get out here."

"Oh, you drove yourself?" the orderly asked.

She shot a glance over her shoulder to see if

the nurse was looking. She wasn't. "Is that the back parking lot?"

"You got it." The orderly accepted the detour easily.

Maybe too easily, Kara thought as they approached the exit—the uncomfortably dark exit.

"You want me to wheel you right to your car?" he asked.

"No!" Kara hauled down her voice. "Here's fine. Thank you."

Two seconds later, the orderly was already halfway back up the hall as she hovered inside the doorway scanning the poorly lit back lot. She dug into her pocket for her cell phone, except…did she really want to hang around here waiting for Ray if maniac nurse had called goons to nab her on sight?

Two blocks. She could run that in under five minutes. Clutching her phone, she yanked up her hoodie and plunged into the misty darkness.

The slap of footsteps on the wet pavement sounded behind her.

Heart pounding, she quickened her pace.

The sound got louder, closer.

Breaking into a sprint, she glanced over her shoulder. The shadowy figure behind her abruptly stopped. "Whew," Kara breathed, and then slammed into a solid wall of muscle.

Powerful hands clamped around her upper arms. "I gotcha."

TWO

"Kara?" Jake tightened his hold on the terri-fied woman and glanced at the man who'd been following her. Or had seemed to be. He'd since veered down a row of parked cars and appeared to be unlocking one.

"Oh, Jake. It's you." Raindrops streaked Kara's face, looking too much like tears, but the relief that oozed from her words gave him a kick of pleasure.

He'd hoped to run into her here. Not this way. But he wasn't complaining. "Who was that guy?" He hitched his chin in the direction of the man who'd since climbed into a nondescript sedan.

"I—" Kara caught her breath. "I don't know. I thought he was following me and I…I guess I got spooked." She suddenly tensed, backed up a step. "What are you doing here?"

The lights in the hospital's back parking lot did little to push back the darkness, but this close, he could see wariness replace the relief that had been in her eyes moments ago. Still, he thought better of releasing his hold just yet. "One of my men was brought in for smoke inhalation. I came by to check on him."

And on you.

But she didn't need to know that. What were the doctors thinking releasing her so soon? She didn't look ready to face the night with no home to return to. He was convinced that she knew more about the fire than she was saying. And one way or the other, he needed to coax her into telling him everything she knew.

"Oh." She shot a nervous glance over her shoulder but didn't make another attempt to escape his hold. "I'm sorry. I hope your friend will be okay."

That much, at least, he believed. But this latest fire had all the earmarks of being another of their elusive firebug's. That made five in the past nine weeks. Four of those had been on his watch, and this was the only one they'd come close to getting a lead on the culprit…in the person of Kara Grant.

Jake gritted his teeth. His gut told him she wasn't the firebug, as he'd initially suspected, but no way was her wild-eyed panic merely a post-traumatic reaction to a random attack. She thought she'd been deliberately targeted.

If he hadn't been sure of it before, he was now. As far as he was concerned, she was the key to nailing this guy. He steered her to an overhang, out of the rain. "I volunteered to help with the fire investigation."

"Wow, that's really nice of you."

"So I'll probably see you again."

Kara fussed with the zipper on her hoodie, clearly reluctant to meet his gaze.

"This guy needs to be stopped, Kara. He's gotten away with torching places across the county for too long."

Her attention snapped to his face. "You think tonight's fire was the work of a serial arsonist?" An odd note of hope rang in her voice, as if she knew it was personal, but hoped it wasn't.

"Yes, didn't the sheriff tell you? That's why if you think of anything else you heard or saw tonight, we need to know." He cocked his head. Something about her expression seemed eerily familiar. He blinked, recalling the day his mother-in-law had shown up on their doorstep, the first time she'd left her abusive husband.

Was that why Kara had resisted being photographed?

Jake's concern for her ballooned. He pulled a card from his wallet and jotted his number on the back. "That's my cell number. Call me if you think of anything that might help. Or if you need anything, okay?"

Nodding, she tucked the card into her hip

pocket. "Sure." Her gaze strayed to a car pulling out of the parking lot—the car of the guy who'd seemed to be following her. As it disappeared around the corner, her shoulders relaxed. "I really need to go now. My friend's still waiting for me."

Jake caught her hand. "Hey, let me give you a lift."

The wild-eyed look returned as she jerked free of his hold. "That's okay. I can walk."

He raised his palms to assure her he meant no harm. "What kind of gentleman would I be if I let you walk in this weather?"

Doubt flickered in her eyes.

Had an abusive husband put it there? His gaze flicked to her bare ring finger. Except that a missing ring didn't mean anything. He traced his own ringless finger, remembering the Thanksgiving night five years ago that he'd lost his wife. He drew in a deep breath.

After he'd lifted Kara into the ambulance earlier, he hadn't been able to walk away as he normally would have. Not when her gaze kept straying his way, as if he was the one person who made her feel safe. His wife used to tease him about his hero complex.

Except in the end, of all people, it'd been her he hadn't been able to save.

"I prefer to walk, thanks," Kara said, already backing away.

"Are you sure you're okay?"

Her tiny smile nuzzled into his chest as palpably as his five-year-old son at bedtime. "Yes. Thank you for your concern." With that she ducked around the side of the building and jogged toward the street.

For half a second, he debated letting her go, but if he was right about Kara's situation being the same as his mother-in-law's, he couldn't just walk away. Not when his mother-in-law's fatal mistake had been agreeing to meet the abusive husband she'd fled from. Bracing himself against the staggering regret that piggybacked that thought, Jake hopped into his truck and followed Kara. He tried to stay far enough back to not spook her, but twice she threw a glance over her shoulder and quickened her pace. When she veered into the coffee shop's parking lot, he pulled onto the side street flanking it.

The rain had stopped, but that didn't make the dimly lit shop, with its tired awning and ancient-looking specials scrawled on the front window, look any more inviting.

A lone guy, shaggy hair, leather jacket, sat at a booth next to the window, his back to it as he chatted with the waitress. Was he the *friend* she was supposed to meet? What kind of jerk wouldn't walk the two blocks to meet her at the hospital?

Her steps faltered as she neared the door.

Jake gripped his truck's door handle, ready to move in if she needed help.

The waitress and customer looked Kara's way as she pushed through the shop's door. Without moving any closer, Kara chatted with them a moment, then took a seat at the counter.

Okay, not what he expected. Had she been feeding him a line about meeting a friend here? He scanned the deserted parking lot. Or had her friend given up waiting for her?

Jake released his grip on the door handle and returned his hands to the steering wheel. Maybe he'd let his imagination get the better of him about the danger she was in. For all he knew, she'd been petrified that he was still trying to pin the arson on her.

He could see only her back through the window, but there was no mistaking the way her shoulders slumped. If her *friend* didn't show soon, he could happen in and offer her a lift. With her house burned, she was going to need to find a place to crash for the night. Hadyn didn't have a hotel, and the only one in Stalwart was likely already booked solid for the holiday. And chances were she hadn't escaped the house with her wallet to pay for a cab to get her any farther.

His cell phone rang. "Hi, Mom. Is everything okay with Tommy?"

"Yes, but he insists you said he could wait up for you. How much longer do you think you'll be?"

Jake blew out a breath. As much as he wanted to make sure Kara was really meeting a friend, his son was his first priority, especially tonight of all nights. "Not much longer. I have to check in on one of my men at the hospital and then I'll head straight home." He started his truck and gave Kara one last glance.

The smile she'd given him when she'd thanked him for caring flickered through his thoughts. Given time, he was pretty sure he could coax her to be more forthcoming. Except they didn't have any time to spare.

Up until tonight, their arsonist had struck every other Friday, and he'd torched vacant buildings, abandoned sheds. The only lives threatened had been firefighters'. But tonight, the stakes had escalated.

Kara could have died in that fire.

With lights on in the upper part of the house and her car in the driveway, there was no way the guy who torched the place couldn't have known that *someone* was in there. But did he know that someone was Kara?

Where was the marshal? Kara had almost lost her supper when two steps into the coffee shop she'd yelped, "I made it," and the man who'd turned in the booth to gape at her had been a stranger. Part of her had wanted to bolt right back outside, but instead she'd shaken her hood off her head and griped about how wet it was outside, then sank onto one of the stools lining the long counter.

The waitress pushed a coffee-stained menu her way. "What can I get you, sugar?" she drawled, sounding as if she belonged in Texas, not Washington State.

Kara dug into her pocket and came up with a wrinkled buck and a couple of quarters. "Uh, just a coffee, please. Black." She pushed the money across the counter as the waitress filled a white mug from a pot that had probably been sitting around all day. "I guess you haven't had too many people in tonight?" Kara fished.

"Not a soul until Bruiser—" the waitress hitched her elbow in the other patron's direction "—stopped by to keep me company." Returning the coffeepot to the burner, she glanced at the clock. "You only just made it. Be closing in twenty minutes."

Kara swallowed a mouthful of the bitter brew. *Not a soul?* She twisted on her stool and scanned the dimly lit lot through the main windows. Would Ray have waited for her outside? "No one all night?" she clarified.

"Nope, not since before supper."

Before the fire, too. What did she do now? He should've been here hours ago. Did he get her message and go straight to the hospital? But then why not phone to let her know?

The waitress deposited the money in the till, then looked curiously at a business card and pushed it back across the counter. "This must be yours." She resumed her conversation with Bruiser.

Kara glanced at the card, realized it was the one Jake had given her and breathed in his lingering scent—as calming and steadfast as a pine forest. He'd looked ruggedly handsome in his jeans and flannel-lined jacket. She traced her thumb over the number he'd scrawled on the card. Had he volunteered to assist the fire investigation so he'd have an excuse to see her again?

If only…things were different.

If wishes were horses, beggars would ride.

How many times had she recited that nursery rhyme to her students to encourage them to act instead of sitting around dreaming?

If only she were free to act…

She stuffed the card back into her pocket and twisted the mug of coffee between her chilled hands, the brew as black as her future seemed. As much as she wanted to believe that she'd merely been the victim of a random arsonist attack, she didn't think she'd imagined the guy in the parking lot coming after her, or that nurse's less-than-subtle attempt to stab her with a needle.

And what made her think Jake could be trusted?

Seemed way too convenient how he kept showing up when she was in trouble, acting like someone she could depend on. Hadn't she once thought Clark was a guy she could depend on?

Look how wrong that perception had turned out. They'd dated for six months, but he'd walked away the minute the Boston paper had hit the stands with a front-page story on an unidentified kindergarten teacher who'd exposed an illegal adoption ring. Unidentified, that was, if the reader didn't look too closely at the grainy picture of her that accompanied the article. Worse than that, he'd all but said "I told you so" after a bomb had nearly killed her later that same day. He'd never cared about her. Only himself. Just like her father.

No, Jake would turn out to be like every other man in her life—never there when she needed him most.

Not even the marshal showed up when needed. And he was paid to protect her!

She closed her eyes and let out a bone-weary sigh. *Lord, can I count on You?*

She sipped her coffee and slipped her phone from her pocket. No missed messages.

The coffee curdled in her stomach. She was wet and cold, had no money, no ID, and in twenty minutes—correction, seventeen minutes—she'd have nowhere to go. The last place she wanted to show her face again was at the hospital. The whole way to the coffee shop, she'd had the creepy feeling someone was following her. She glanced at the window and shrank at the realization of how easily someone could be watching her even now. The thought of going back out there without the marshal made her stomach lurch.

She thumbed a text message to Ray. I'm at the coffee shop. Where are you?

She set the phone on the counter and forced down another gulp of coffee as the clock's second hand ticked its way around the clock face. After four minutes went by, she punched in his number. It immediately went to voice mail. Maybe he'd been trying to call her. She waited another three minutes. Checked her messages.

Nothing.

The screen on a small TV mounted in the corner above the counter flicked to an image of a bloated body being pulled from the Charles River in Boston. She choked on her coffee as the camera zoomed in on the man's face. She couldn't believe it! It was the man she'd seen collecting money for the child he'd handed over. If the adoption ring would kill its own employee…

Her heart hammered in her chest as she punched Ray's number into her phone again. Again, it went straight to voice mail, and a scarier thought gripped her. What if they'd gotten to him, too? Gotten his phone? Heard her messages?

They would've guessed she was at the hospital anyway, but now they'd know she was at a coffee shop, and there weren't that many of those in a town the size of Hadyn. Not to mention, they'd have her number, be able to track her phone.

She turned it over in her hand. She had to get rid of it.

Snatching up her spoon, she pried open the back of the phone, pulled the battery. But what if that wasn't enough? She had no idea how GPS tracking worked. She slipped into the bathroom, tossed the phone into the trash can, stuffed crumpled swaths of paper towel in over top.

Only…now, Ray had no way to reach her.

It couldn't be helped. She finger-combed her hair, scrubbed smudges of soot from her face. When she was far away from here, she'd find a pay phone and try calling him again.

Except what if they were already outside waiting for her?

A high-pitched scream pierced the air.

"Down on the floor," a deep male voice barked, followed by the crash of dishes.

Terror squeezed her chest. *Oh, dear God, please don't let them find me.*

THREE

After checking on his injured firefighter in the E.R., Jake hurried back out to his truck to get home to his son. The poor little guy wouldn't be happy to learn his dad had volunteered tomorrow's day off to consult on the arson investigation. The least Jake owed him was some cuddle time tonight. Kara's frightened face flashed through his thoughts as he stopped at the hospital parking lot's exit. He still had an uneasy feeling about the supposed friend she'd gone to meet. It would take only a couple of minutes to stop by the coffee shop to see if he, or she, had shown.

An ambulance whipped out of the next lane and veered across his path, sirens blaring.

Jake glanced after it and his heart rammed into his throat at the sight of swirling emergency lights two blocks down. He peeled his truck out after the ambulance. Cruisers blocked the streets around the coffee shop. Jake slammed the steering wheel. He never should have left Kara there. She'd been too edgy.

Jake screeched to a stop, half on the sidewalk, just outside the roadblock and cut around the cars on foot. Two deputies hauled a handcuffed punk from the asphalt. Another recovered a sawed-off shotgun—*oh, God, please not again.* The deputy waved the paramedics into the shop and Jake raced after them.

Someone slammed him into the side of a cruiser. "You can't go in there."

He strained to see around the deputy who'd body checked him. "My friend's in there." He spotted the sheriff giving orders to one of the deputies outside. "Sheriff, is Kara okay?"

The sheriff headed Jake's way. "This has been one wild night. There must be a full moon behind all those clouds. What are you doing here?"

"Kara was in the shop. Is she okay?"

"The woman from the fire?"

"Yeah." Jake jutted his chin toward the suspect—a mercenary type sporting military fatigues, a shaved head and the muscles to back up his threats. "Is that our arsonist?" And if his guess was right, an ex-husband or ex-boyfriend, too.

"You say she was here?"

Jake's heart jackhammered his ribs. "She's not now? Was there another guy? Did he take her?"

"Slow down." The sheriff waved off the deputy who'd manhandled him and led Jake toward the front door of the shop. "The waitress said there'd been another customer, but that she disappeared before the gunman came in."

"What do you mean *disappeared?*"

"She thought she went to the bathroom. Except she isn't there now. But the window was unlatched."

"So she escaped?" Except that meant she was out there alone. Unprotected. "You need men searching for her. A K-9 unit."

"We don't have one, but trust me, we've got men combing the streets. Seems your first instinct about her at the fire might've been right. Sounds as if she could've been the gunman's accomplice. The waitress said she'd been texting just before the gunman stormed in."

Jake snatched his cell phone from his hip. "You got her number?"

"Yeah." The sheriff flipped open his notebook and recited the number as Jake punched it in.

"Her friend was supposed to meet her here." The phone rang and rang. Voice mail never picked up. He clicked it off. "She's not answering."

The sheriff opened the shop door and motioned to the paramedics tending to a guy on the floor. "That the friend she came to see?"

Jake recognized the victim's leather coat, longish hair from the coffee shop window. At the sight of the man's bloodied face, Jake almost heaved. That could've been Kara.

"He wrestled the gunman to the ground while the waitress called 9-1-1." The sheriff let out a soft clicking sound. "But the gunman got in a couple of nasty gun butts to the head."

Jake hadn't gotten the impression this guy was who Kara came to see, but... "Sounds as though he might've been." Kara had said he'd keep her safe. Apparently she'd been right. Jake hoped.

The sheriff flipped to a fresh page in his notebook. "So what am I supposed to make of the woman being at two of my crime scenes in one night? If she was the target and not the instigator, why didn't she ask for protection?"

Jake's gut tightened. He could think of one reason. Maybe whoever Kara was running from was good at convincing the authorities he was an upstanding guy. Just like his father-in-law. Cop by day, abuser by night.

A waitress hovered over the paramedics, mascara streaking her cheeks.

"You know the victim?" Jake asked her.

She nibbled nervously on her fingernails. "He's my boyfriend."

The sheriff's gaze snapped to Jake. "You sure you've got your facts straight?"

Jake refocused on the waitress. "The customer

you mentioned to the sheriff, was she wearing a dark hoodie, about five-four, shoulder-length brown hair?"

"Yeah." The waitress pulled her fingers away from her mouth, curled her hands into her apron. "She was the only customer I had all night."

"Besides your boyfriend?" Jake clarified.

"Well, yeah."

"Did she talk to him?"

"No. She sat at the counter."

Jake's gaze tracked to the unfinished mug of black coffee, the muddy puddle beneath the stool.

"I got the sense she was waiting for someone."

The sheriff cocked his head toward Jake, lifting a brow.

No, she did not flee a fire to wait for a gunman in a coffee shop. That made no sense at all. Jake maneuvered around the sheriff to talk to the victim on the ground. "Did you know the female customer who came in?"

The guy's eyes fluttered open then closed like leaden curtains.

"Afraid it'll be a few hours before you get any answers out of him," the paramedic said. "We're ready to transport," he added, directing that to the sheriff.

"Go ahead. The scene is secure."

The waitress started for the door, then flailed

her arms helplessly. "I need to go with him, but am I supposed to lock up?"

"The owner is on his way," the sheriff reassured, "but I need you to answer a few more questions before you go. I'll have one of my deputies drive you to the hospital. Okay?"

She gazed forlornly after the disappearing gurney and sank onto a stool. "I already told you everything."

"You'd be surprised what you might've picked up without realizing it." The sheriff clapped Jake on the shoulder. "Thanks for the tip on the woman. I'll be in touch about the fire investigation." And just like that Jake was dismissed.

Outside the shop, Jake scanned the dark streets, beyond the swirl of emergency lights. *Lord, please let them find Kara safe.*

He zipped his jacket against the fine rain that had started up again, like the niggling feeling he'd let another woman down this Thanksgiving. Five years ago, his gut had told him to take his wife to the E.R. in case the bleeding wasn't normal postbirth hemorrhaging. Instead he'd let her sway him into believing she'd be fine.

As he'd done tonight.

He climbed into his truck and slammed the door on the memory. *Lord, what is wrong with me? She was obviously in trouble, no matter what she said. Why'd I walk away?* Then. Now.

At the sound of Beethoven's Fifth—the ringtone reserved for his parents—chiming from his hip, he snatched up his phone. "Is Tommy okay?"

"Yes, but we'll soon be heading to bed ourselves. Wanted to say if you were going to be much later, you might as well just leave him here for the night."

And face an empty house alone? Not tonight. "I'm on my way now." There was nothing more he could do here.

With one last glance toward the suspect warming a seat in the back of a cruiser, Jake hiked back to his truck. If his guess was right, and this was the guy Kara had been afraid of, at least she'd be safe now.

The thought didn't ease the hundred-pound weight parked on his chest. He pulled a U-turn onto the empty street and headed home. He was a firefighter. His job was to put out fires, rescue victims. Chasing after Kara at the scene had been above and beyond. So why did he feel as if he hadn't done nearly enough?

Glancing at the snapshot pinned to his dashboard, of April cuddling their newborn son, Jake tamped down the urge to go out looking for Kara and leaned on the gas.

A thump sounded in the bed of the pickup. Must've missed a firewood log when he'd emptied the couple of cords he'd picked up yesterday.

Seemed as if he was missing things left, right and center these days.

If not for wanting to try to catch Kara at the hospital, and hopefully a lead on their arsonist, he never would've let the chief of Hadyn's volunteer crew convince him to leave the rest of the cleanup to them. What if they destroyed key evidence?

The cops didn't call firefighters evidence destroyers for no reason.

Ten minutes later, he stopped at the intersection leading to his street and clicked on his turn signal. As he touched the gas, a shadowy movement in the rearview mirror caught his attention. He punched the brakes and more than just a thump sounded from the back of his truck bed. That had sounded like a yelp.

He rammed his stick shift into Park, grabbed a crowbar from under the seat and jumped from his truck. He clanked down the tailgate and yanked on the tarp bunched over a hump in the far corner. "Kara?"

She shrank into the corner of the rain-slicked truck bed, drenched and sickly white under the glare of the streetlight.

"What are you doing back here? Get into the cab before you catch your death!" His throat closed on that last order.

Instead of scrambling to obey, she shrank

deeper into the corner, tugging what little she could of the tarp back over her body.

Jake's fury and confusion, and emotions he didn't have time to identify, seeped out in a frustrated sigh. "Kara, I won't hurt you." Her gaze darted to the crowbar poised over his head, and he dropped it onto the truck bed. "Please, come out of the rain. They caught the gunman. He can't hurt you anymore."

She edged toward the tailgate, ignoring the hand he offered. Well, not exactly ignoring. Her gaze was fixed on it as if she feared he might grab her.

Biting back the questions and assurances pressing at his throat, he pulled his hand to his side.

The tightness around her mouth eased as she quickly slid off the tailgate and headed toward the passenger door.

Giving her the space she seemed to need, he took a moment to latch the tailgate. "There's a blanket in the cab. Wrap it around yourself. I'll call the sheriff. Let him know you're safe."

Silence.

"Kara?" He came around the truck to give her a hand, but she was gone. "Kara!"

Hedges on the other side of the ditch rustled.

He grabbed a flashlight and took off after her. She'd been okay until he mentioned the sheriff. And he'd told her they'd caught the gunman. Cop or no cop, he'd be warming a jail cell. So why run now?

Unless she wasn't innocent.

If she'd been smart, she'd have kept on running the instant she jumped out of that washroom window and not stopped until she reached Seattle, someplace where she could blend in with thousands of other faceless people and no one would ever find her. Only...

Her handler wouldn't have been able to find her either.

Jake's flashlight beam arced over the yard to her left.

She ducked behind a wrecked car at the back of the neighboring yard. Her hand squished something on the ground that she didn't want to contemplate. Mud seeped over the tops of her shoes, soaked through her already sopping jeans. A brisk wind teased up the back of her shirt, sending more chills through her shivering limbs. What was she going to do? She couldn't exactly call the marshal's office to find out if the bad guys had gotten to Ray. Witness security files were top secret. How many times had he drilled that into her?

"Kara," Jake called. "C'mon, I want to help you."

His pleading tone tugged at a cold, lonely place in her heart desperate to believe him. Never mind how he always seemed to show up when the trouble started. If he'd wanted to hurt her, he never would've let her walk away from the hospital. Right?

She swallowed the bile rising to her throat. Unless he was the one she'd sensed following her to the coffee shop, the one who'd sent in the gunman.

Jake's voice drifted farther away, and she peeked over the back of the rusted jalopy. *Please, Lord, let him give up looking.* No matter how concerned Jake sounded, she couldn't trust him.

If things fall apart, don't trust anyone. They'll pretend to be on your side, pretend to want to help you, pretend to be taking you to safety just long enough to get you somewhere secluded.

Her stomach pitched at the memory of the marshal's warning. Not that this place was secluded. Or that Jake had known she was in the truck when he'd driven here for that matter. If she'd known it was his truck, she never would've jumped in it.

She couldn't afford to take any chances. She tugged her sleeves down over her icy hands and pushed to her feet. A few more hours. That was all she needed. Tomorrow she'd go to the fail-safe meet site. That was where Ray would look for her next, and if something *had* happened to him, that was where his office would send another marshal to take care of her—someone who'd know the code phrase they'd agreed on.

Behind her a yard light blinked on. The back door creaked open.

Holding her breath, she edged toward the next yard. If the owner had let out a dog, she was—

"Kara!" Jake's voice came louder again.

He was coming back! She darted in the opposite direction.

A barking dog raced toward her, yelped when he hit the end of his chain and got jerked off his feet. An instant later, his barking veered to the other end of the yard. *Jake.*

She tightened her fists and pumped her arms to drive herself faster. The dearth of streetlights hid her from view, but made running treacherous. She jumped over toys and tree limbs and— "Ah!" Her foot pinged a large can, sent it clattering over the rough ground. She stumbled, her ankle twisting.

"Kara, wait." Jake's flashlight speared her back.

Ignoring the pain screaming through her ankle, she took off again at a sprint. She veered between two houses, praying she didn't run into anything else. Oh, why did it have to be Jake's truck she'd jumped into?

The dog she'd heard barking outside the coffee shop after the police showed up probably hadn't even been a police dog, but all she'd been able to think to do was run through the puddles to mask her scent and get away. His truck's sudden appearance had seemed like a godsend. Why couldn't Jake have just been some rubbernecker who'd move on after a few minutes of gawking?

"Kara, listen to me." Jake's footfalls pounded behind her, but the stamina she'd gained from her daily five-mile runs kept her ahead of him. "Kara," he huffed, clearly tiring.

Wet and cold and hungry, she forced her mind off the fatigue tugging at her own limbs. *Lord, please let him run out of steam before I do.*

"If you didn't set the fire, you have no reason to run," Jake called between heavy breaths. "The police will protect you from whoever you're afraid of. Was that guy an ex-boyfriend? Your husband?"

Husband? Was that what he thought? She tripped over the curb as she chanced a glance over her shoulder.

Jake burst from between the houses just as she recovered her balance. His gaze slammed into hers. The dim light couldn't mask the concern she saw flickering in his eyes. He slowed to a sedate approach, patted the air with the hand not holding a flashlight as if she were a skittish colt. "I can help you, Kara. My wife's dad was an abuser, I—"

The sound of a siren broke his spell. He'd called

the police. She gulped in a lungful of air. "If you really want to help me, Jake, forget you ever saw me." She turned on her heel and ran.

"Kara!"

Blinding headlights blipped on and she froze. Her heart jammed in her throat as the lights sped toward her. *Oh, God, I'm going to die.*

Hurled into the hedges on the other side of the road, her body exploded in agony. Then everything went black.

FOUR

Headlights swerved over them. Brakes screeched. Jake shielded Kara's head with his arms, his body pinning her to the muddy ground. He prayed the out-of-control car didn't barrel into the ditch and onto them.

Suddenly, everything stilled, headlights shrouding the ground in an unearthly glow. Jake tensed at the click of a car door opening. Was the driver coming to make sure they were okay? Or to finish them off?

He eased off Kara, gently swept her rain-drenched hair from her face. "Hey, you with me?" he whispered.

Her eyes blinked open. "I'm not dead?"

Not yet. He shot a glance over his shoulder at the flashlight bobbing toward them. "Can you get up? Did I hurt you?" He'd rammed her hard enough to break a few bones if she'd landed the wrong way, but better that than being crushed by a car.

She wiggled her arms, then her legs. "Just bruised, I think."

"Hey, Jake, is that you? Are you okay?" The flashlight beamed his face.

He shielded his eyes against the blinding glare. "Sherri? What are you doing here?"

"What am I doing here? What are you doing here? I was on my way home when I saw your truck abandoned on the end of your street the headlights still on and the door half-opened. Who—?" She swerved the flashlight beam to Kara still lying on the ground. "Kara?" Sherri sprang into action, sliding to her knees at Kara's side. "Are you okay? I didn't hit you did I?" She palpated Kara's arms. "You came out of nowhere. I—"

"What were you doing driving down the road without your headlights on?" Jake growled, taking over her flashlight so she could see Kara better.

"I heard you yelling. I thought you needed help. What were you doing running after her anyway?"

"Never mind that for now!"

Sherri lifted an eyebrow at his sharp tone, but thankfully let it go. "Like I was saying," she continued, moving on to Kara's legs. "When I saw a flashlight beam bounce off the trees, I turned off my headlights to pinpoint where it was coming from. Then you guys ran right out in front of me!"

"I'm fine." Kara pushed to her elbows and edged warily away from Sherri's touch, looking anything but fine. Her clothes were soaked and every inch of her was covered in mud.

"We should get her to the hospital," Jake said to Sherri.

Kara scrambled to her feet. "I don't need to go to the hospital. I'm fine."

"Okay." Jake patted the air, urging her to calm down. The last thing he wanted to do was make her run again. "My parents' house is around the corner. Let's at least get you out of this rain and into some dry clothes." He nodded his chin toward her muddy bandage. "That bandage will need changing, too, if you don't want to risk infection."

"Good idea," Sherri said. "The hospital is a zoo tonight anyway what with that guy at the coffee shop shanking two deputies."

"What?" Jake and Kara shrieked at the same time.

"I guess you haven't heard. This gunman tried to rob the coffee shop. The police arrested him, but then he pulled some kind of blade on them and got away."

Kara's terrified gaze slammed into Jake's.

"It's going to be okay," he murmured, pulling her into his arms. To his relief, she accepted their protective shelter. "He's not going to find you. Okay?" Jake whispered close to her ear. He could feel her heart hammering against his chest. Tucking her close to his side, he turned to Sherri. "Drive us to my folks. Then you can bring my dad back to pick up my truck. Okay?"

"Yeah, sure." Her curious look said she was waiting for an explanation.

He ignored it and guided Kara to the backseat of Sherri's Ford Escort. "My mom's a retired nurse," he babbled to Kara, sliding in beside her and tucking the blanket he found on the seat around her. "She can take care of that bandage and give you some dry clothes."

Kara nodded mutely, and he worried that she was going into shock again. She was so cold, so wet. Questions torpedoed his mind, demanding answers. Answers that might help the sheriff track the gunman down. But a quiet voice inside his head told him not to push. Not yet. Or she'd run again, before he could help her.

Thankfully, Sherri seemed to sense that now was not the time to get her questions answered either, because for once, she stopped grilling him. She turned the heater on full blast, even though they'd be in his folks' driveway before it blew anything warmer than tepid air.

Kara must've felt she owed him an explanation, because as Sherri turned onto his street, she said,

"My friend wasn't at the coffee shop like he was supposed to be."

"No?"

She swallowed. "I was waiting for him, had just gone to the washroom, when that robber came in. But I don't know him. It's not like you think."

"It's not?"

She shook her head, sneaked a glance at the rearview mirror, where Sherri's eyes were fixed on them. Jake hadn't noticed that his cousin had already parked and turned off the engine. Part of him wished the house was a little farther away so Kara might not have clammed up, but he hazarded a question anyway. "Then why'd you hide in my truck? Why didn't you talk to the police?"

"I was scared. I'm sorry. I shouldn't have involved you." She pushed off the blanket. "I'll go."

He caught the edge of the blanket and wrapped it back around her. "Not a chance. I've worried about you enough for one night."

Her unusual brown eyes momentarily widened, and then slipped shut, her impossibly long lashes sweeping her cheeks. "I've caused you a lot of trouble." She lifted her gaze, but it didn't make it to his. She stared at Tommy's face pressed to the kitchen window. "You should be home with your family." Her voice broke on the word *family,* sounding hollow and empty and utterly alone.

"Do you have family nearby where you could stay?" he ventured.

She shook her head.

"Then it's settled. Sherri, wait here. I'll send Dad out to go with you for my truck." Jake opened the car door and hurried around to Kara's side. By the time his mom helped her get cleaned up, Dad would be back, and maybe together they could get some answers. With forty-three years in the sheriff's department, ten of those as sheriff, who better than his dad to coax her to let them in on what was really going on?

Tommy waved eagerly from the door, and Kara's evasive answers settled in a hard lump in the pit of Jake's stomach. She might be telling the truth about not knowing the gunman, but that didn't mean he or the arsonist hadn't been targeting Kara. Did he really want to bring that danger so close to home?

Close to Tommy?

Kara climbed from the car and, as if she'd read his thoughts, said, "My purse burned in the fire, or else I'd stay in a hotel. But if this town has a homeless shelter, I—"

"I'm not leaving you at a shelter. My folks have a spare room you can use." He muffled his reflexive gulp as Tommy opened the door for them. *Lord, I'm going with my gut this time. Please don't let me be wrong.*

* * *

Kara surveyed the welcoming glow beaming from the windows of the wood-clad two story, still uncertain if agreeing to come here had been a good idea. Except that bunking at Jake's parents' place had to be safer than sleeping under a bridge somewhere. After all, Jake could've turned her in and he hadn't. That had to count for something. That and the pride in his voice when he threw a wide grin to the boy waiting for them on the porch and said, "That's my son, Tommy." Surely a hit man didn't invite a victim to meet his family, let alone risk his life to save her from being hit by a car.

Jake scaled the porch steps in two long strides and swept his son into a wet, muddy bear hug.

Kara's heart climbed to her throat. It was the kind of elated reunion she'd hoped her testimony and photographs would bring to the parents of the infant she'd seen being sold. She edged back toward the car. "I thought this was your parents' house." She shouldn't be here. What if the bad guys found her here? Threatened Jake's son?

Jake smiled at her over Tommy's shoulder, but she didn't miss the worry that pinched his forehead. "It's my folks' place. Tommy and I live next door. I'm widowed, so my mom watches him when I'm at work." He nuzzled his son's neck. "Right, sport?"

"Right!"

A woman appeared at the door and took in their drenched, muddy state with a gasp. "Oh, my. What happened?" She corralled Kara inside before Jake had even finished his explanation that thankfully didn't include any mention of the gunman at the coffee shop.

An adorable goldendoodle bounded across the kitchen floor and planted his paws on Kara.

"Well, hello!" A happy bubble gurgled up her chest.

"That's Rusty," Tommy announced.

Jake grabbed Rusty's collar and tugged him down to a sitting position. "My parents thought he'd be a good companion for Tommy, but they let him break every rule in the book."

"Maybe I can help. I—" Kara cut off the stupid offer by kneeling down and burying her face in the dog's curly fur. She missed her dog so badly. The marshal had told her to become a cat person, said she'd been too active in the dog-training community to risk the association.

Except the bad guys had found her anyway.

Tears leaked from her eyes, prompting sloppy kisses from the sweet dog and a soft pat on the back from Jake's even sweeter son.

While she asked Tommy about his dog, Jake told his parents that she needed a place to stay. The next thing she knew, Jake's mom swept her up the stairs, turned on the tub's hot water and pressed a fuzzy terry robe and comfy-looking old gym suit onto her as she shooed her toward the steamy bathroom. Kara was just starting to think that maybe God had been watching out for her tonight after all when she caught sight of Jake speaking with his dad at the bottom of the stairs.

From his dad's grim expression, she guessed that Jake had given him the lowdown on what happened. He'd probably ask her to leave as soon as she finished her bath. Or worse, call the sheriff to come get her.

Mrs. Steele pulled the door closed. "Take all the time you need, Kara. I'll warm up soup and make you hot chocolate to chase the rest of that chill away. Then we'll take care of rebandaging that arm."

Kara locked the bathroom door and stood in front of the mirror. Her once long blond hair hung in bedraggled mousy brown strands, reminding her again why she shouldn't be here. There was no way that gunman's appearance had been a random robbery. Just like she didn't believe the fire was the work of a serial arsonist. Whoever was behind the adoption ring probably wanted to make it look as if she died in a random way so the police couldn't pin her death on them, too.

If she was smart, she'd quickly change into the dry clothes and sneak out the bathroom window for the second time tonight. Only—she leaned over the toilet to look outside—this window was fifteen feet off the ground and her shoes were downstairs, sitting next to the side door.

A giant oak stood beside the driveway, a few leaves still clinging to its branches. A lone wooden swing dangled from a sturdy limb, swaying warily.

Jake's dad appeared outside and hurried toward Sherri's car. If Sherri heard her explanation to Jake in the backseat, Kara didn't want to think about what conclusions she and Mr. Steele would draw about her. If they started talking to anyone else, she might never get away.

Kara quickly slipped into the tub, being careful to keep her burned arm above the water. She breathed a contented sigh as the warm water enveloped her. She dared not stay too long, but at least she could ward off the chill that had seeped to her bones before she climbed into the clean, dry clothes Mrs. Steele had provided.

She closed her eyes, unable to remember a bath ever feeling so good. Her left hip and shoulder ached where they'd slammed into the ground. But if not for Jake's lightning-fast reflexes, she might not be here at all. Wrapping her unburned arm around her waist, she nestled into the memory of how safe she'd felt in his embrace. Clark would never have risked running in front of a car to save

her, as Jake had tonight. Even with a son waiting for him at home, Jake hadn't hesitated for a
second.

She smiled at the memory of Tommy's understanding pat on her back as she'd sobbed into
Rusty's fur, swamped by the memory of her beloved pup. He'd saved her life by tearing into
the packaged bomb the adoption ring had clearly
meant for her, but her life as Nicole Redman had
ended with his. Looking into Tommy's empathetic gaze as she hugged his dog, she'd scarcely
resisted the urge to hug him, too. She missed her
kindergarten kids so much.

At the slam of a vehicle door, she grabbed a
towel and jumped from the tub. Jake must've
called the sheriff after all. She peeked over the
windowsill and immediately jerked back at the
sight of Mr. Steele glancing toward it. Was he
contemplating calling the sheriff? Had he already?

She quickly toweled herself dry and pulled on
the borrowed clothes. If they hadn't called the
sheriff, maybe she'd be able to bide her time until
just before dawn, then sneak out and head for the
truck stop on the highway between Hadyn and
Stalwart—the last-resort meet site she'd arranged
with the marshal when she first moved here.

She could probably jog the distance in half an
hour. If they'd already notified the sheriff, she

didn't know what she'd do. With her hand on the doorknob, she closed her eyes. *Lord, guide me. I don't know who I can trust.*

A scratch followed by a whine jolted her attention back to the door. The instant she opened it, Rusty leaned into her leg, then accompanied her downstairs. The comforting smell of hot cocoa lured her toward the kitchen.

"Looks as though you've made a friend." Mrs. Steele set a steaming mug on the dining table. "Come sit." The table was in an open-concept area adjoining the family room, and as Kara sat, she noticed Jake in a recliner, reading a picture book to Tommy snuggled against his broad chest. Jake's rumbly voice did funny things to her heart, and she couldn't help but smile at the heartwarming picture they made.

"He's asleep," Kara whispered, and didn't know what to make of the answering twinkle in Jake's eyes as he finished the story anyway.

He closed the book. "I promised him I'd read it all," Jake explained.

Something inside Kara shifted at the matter-of-fact statement, at the affectionate way he tousled the boy's hair. A man who kept his word was a rarity in her experience. She wanted to ask him if he always kept it, but said instead, "Tommy's very lucky to have you." Not lucky. *Blessed.*

At the disarming intensity of Jake's cobalt-blue

eyes, her pulse quickened. He studied her face, his gaze a physical touch that lingered on her eyes, her hair, her cheeks, before dipping to her lips.

She diverted her attention to her mug of cocoa, her hands trembling for reasons she refused to acknowledge, except that she suddenly regretted the way she'd need to leave here in the morning.

Jake brought Tommy back over to his folks' place just after seven the next morning and found his mom baking muffins in the kitchen. "Kara still asleep?" The sky had started to lighten, but he hoped Kara would sleep well past dawn so he could get in some investigation time at the scene of the fire before needing to worry about what she might do next.

"Yes." Mom's gaze flicked to Tommy as if she wanted to say more.

Jake squeezed his son's shoulder. "Why don't you take Rusty into the backyard for a few minutes?"

Mom shook her head. "I'm not sure Rusty will come down. He's been glued to Kara's side all night." She jutted her chin toward the stairs as she plopped muffin dough into tins. "See for yourself."

"Stay with Gran," Jake told Tommy, then padded upstairs and glanced around the partially open door of the guest bedroom.

Rusty lay on the end of Kara's bed, his head resting on her legs, and only his eyes shifted to look at Jake. With a soft murmur that did funny things to his insides, Kara rolled onto her side. Her eyes didn't open, and for the first time since he met her last night, she looked at peace, with her soft hair framing her heart-shaped face, no wariness creasing her brow.

He breathed a relieved sigh and padded back downstairs. He'd spent half the night second-guessing whether he'd been an idiot to bring her here without telling the sheriff, let alone to acquiesce to her request that they wait until morning to talk about what happened.

But she'd been so concerned about keeping Tommy from his bed, and had looked bone tired herself, that he hadn't wanted to argue.

"She still asleep?" Mom asked as he returned to the kitchen.

"Yeah. Where's Tommy?"

"He walked down with your dad to the corner store to get the paper."

Jake poured himself a cup of coffee from the pot and leaned against the counter. "So what didn't you want to tell me with Tommy around?"

"I think Kara's more shaken up than she wants to let on." Mom lowered her voice to a whisper. "In the middle of the night, your father heard her scream and ran upstairs to check on her. It was just a bad dream, of course. And she felt terrible at having disturbed him. But…well, you know how it is."

Yeah. He'd relived too many fires in his dreams. Or worse, the night April died. He gulped a mouthful of coffee to mask the bitter taste suddenly burning his throat. "I'll talk to her." Maybe talking through it would help her process everything a little more so she wouldn't end up dreaming about the fire every night. Or whatever else was giving her nightmares. In Sherri's car, she'd said that she didn't have an abusive ex hunting her, but he wasn't sure he believed her.

He downed the last of his coffee and set his mug in the sink. "I need to get to the scene. We're starting at first light. But call me as soon as she wakes. I'll come straight back."

"I'm sure she'll be fine here for a few hours. Although I imagine she'll be anxious to hear what you find, and to know if she can salvage any of her belongings. After you left, she admitted that she didn't have tenant's insurance. And on a janitor's salary, I suspect she doesn't have a lot of savings to draw on."

"Just call me right away, okay?" Jake hurried outside and started his truck as quietly as he could manage, which wasn't all that quiet. He shot a glance to the second-story guest room window. Seeing no movement, he eased the truck out of the driveway and then sped back to Hadyn, a ten-minute drive in good conditions. But that morning's fog slowed him down.

By the time he arrived at the scene, the fire marshal, four other guys and the sheriff were already on-site. He couldn't hold back the groan that ground through his gut as he surveyed what was left of Kara's home—the charcoaled timbers, the wet curtains dangling out the window, the gaping hole where the roof used to be. A hole that looked horribly like her life about now.

Jake approached the fire marshal. "What have you got so far? Does it look like our serial arsonist has stepped up his pace?"

"Not sure yet. We might have a copycat. The master electrician's in there ruling out electrical causes, but the batteries were missing from the smoke detectors and I spoke with the owner last night. She claims she'd put in new batteries at the beginning of the month."

"Which points to a deliberate act."

"Yeah, and based on what the first guys on the scene reported about the color of the flames and the fire's behavior, it definitely sounds as though an accelerant was involved. And it definitely started from inside."

Jake's gut pitched. That meant they'd have a lot more questions for Kara, and they might not be friendly. There'd been no evidence of a break-in before the volunteer crew had kicked open the doors.

"But we might have one break. Apparently a reporter photographed the fire and crowd. He may have caught our firebug watching his handiwork." The fire marshal swept aside what was left of the bushes in the garden at the base of the house. "I asked the sheriff to get copies of the photos. Maybe a face will pop—one you've seen at other fires."

"Not sure I'd be much help there. Too busy fighting fires to watch the crowd." Except last night. He'd inexplicably sensed Kara watching.

Wanting to get back to her ASAP, Jake scrutinized the narrow metal vent in the cement blocks the marshal had exposed. "Did you see any way someone could access the crawl space from outside?"

"Not the crawl space, exactly." The fire marshal led him to the side of the house where the bulk of the damage had occurred and the men were meticulously picking through the layers of what remained. "The owner says there's a cellar under this end of the house."

"And it looks as if that's where the fire started?"

"Yeah, but whoever set it still had to get inside. And he didn't get in through a vent."

Jake surveyed the men still working through the second story of debris, a muscle in his cheek twitching involuntarily at the thought of what they were looking for. Even though they'd been told there was no one else in the house, they had to make sure. It would be hours, maybe days, before they dug down to the fire's source. Jake pulled a jackknife from his pocket and pried off one of the metal grilles ventilating the cellar. He peered through the narrow opening with his penlight. "Get me a Maglite, will ya?"

The marshal pried off a vent at the corner and shone the light through it.

At the sight of candle remnants and a black scorch mark on the floor left behind by the trailer that would have carried the flame, Jake said, "We're looking at the same M.O. as the other fires. Tip the light a little higher."

Jake craned his neck to follow the line. "Yeah, I can see scalding marks where the gasoline ignited." Since candles burned at a rate of an inch an hour, the arsonist likely rigged this after seeing the owner leave with an overnight bag, maybe not realizing she had a tenant.

The fire marshal cursed. "The balloon construction on these old houses makes for perfect conditions for the fire to fly up the walls and become dangerously hot before you know it's even there. No wonder the victim didn't see it coming."

Yeah, the same way his wife's internal hemorrhaging following Tommy's birth had caught them unaware. Thrown by the direction his thoughts had veered, Jake clicked off his pen-light and sat back on his heels. The anniversary of April's death was two days ago, which had to be why he was comparing it to Kara's situation. At least it looked as if, maybe, Kara had just been in the wrong place at the wrong time after all.

"We've got to catch this guy," the fire marshal said grimly. "Fires like these are the hardest and deadliest to fight. You can never predict where they might erupt, especially if he starts stringing trailers to multiple pools of accelerant."

"Yeah." Jake's gaze strayed to where he'd first spotted Kara hiding in the hedges. "I'd much rather fight what I can see coming."

FIVE

At the aroma of baking, Kara jackknifed out of bed. Rusty sat up and watched her expectantly. Misty light streamed through the window. No, no, no. She'd deliberately not pulled the shades so she wouldn't sleep in. How was she going to get away now, with everyone awake?

She stuffed her legs into the track pants Mrs. Steele had loaned her last night and pulled on Jake's high school athletics jacket over the T-shirt she'd worn to bed. She winced as the sleeve grazed her bandaged burn. Mrs. Steele had been so kind last night, taking the time to clean and rebandage her arm. Kara hated to up and run away…in borrowed clothes, no less.

Rusty, who'd been tilting his head at her muttering, suddenly plopped his head between his paws and looked at her disappointedly.

"I can't help it," she whispered. "I have no idea where she put my clothes!" Kara rummaged through the box of old clothes Mrs. Steele had left for her and found a pair of socks. Rusty seemed to take that as a hopeful sign. He jumped from the bed and pranced to the door. Okay, clearly there was no way she could just sneak out with the dog watching her. Maybe Jake had been fibbing about the dog not being trained. She wouldn't put it past him to have ordered Rusty to make sure she didn't leave.

The dog plopped his curly rump on the ground at the bedroom door and gave her another head-tilted look.

"Yeah, play innocent." She affectionately tousled the dog's ears. "But I'm on to you."

The dog raced down the stairs ahead of her, eliminating any last hope of making her escape before being spotted. Tommy raced around the corner from the kitchen. "She's up!" He disappeared and reappeared as she reached the bottom step. "I made this for you. To feel better." He presented her with a colorful turkey made of construction paper—the kind she would've had her students make if her life hadn't been ripped away from her. She imagined the Thanksgiving party her students would have had at school this past week and longed for another chance to be a part of that.

Tears pricked her eyes as she sank onto the bottom step. "Thank you. It's beautiful." She choked out the words, feeling a little silly at how affected she was by such a simple gesture. While holidays weren't as big a deal in her family as she would have liked, she hated that she hadn't been able to be with them to celebrate, not even able to call.

Tommy patted her knee. "I fell off my bike last week and scraped my arm." He jutted out his elbow for her perusal. "So I know how ya feel."

Rusty planted his rump on the stair and leaned heavily against her, offering his moral support, too.

She grinned and hugged them both. "Thank you. You two sure know how to make a girl feel better."

Mrs. Steele's beaming face peeked around the corner. "Muffins are ready if you're hungry."

Tommy grabbed Kara's hand and tugged her toward the kitchen. "C'mon, you'll love Gran's muffins. She makes them to cheer me up, too."

Kara gulped back the guilt that burbled into her throat at the feel of Tommy's small hand in hers. The last thing she wanted to do was hurt a child, and he wasn't going to understand why she'd leave without saying goodbye. She never should have come here.

Pasting on a smile that she was pretty sure Mrs. Steele saw right through, Kara stepped into the kitchen. At least there was no sign of Jake or his father around. She almost asked after them, but thought better of it. She'd have an easier time coming up with an excuse Tommy and his grand-mother would believe than one Jake and his father would.

"Why don't you take Rusty out back for a bit?" Mrs. Steele urged Tommy as she set a mug of coffee in front of Kara at the table. "Give Miss Kara a chance to eat her breakfast."

Tommy raced for the door. Pausing on the threshold, he turned back to Kara. "When you're done eating, I'll show you the tricks I learned him."

Kara drew back the mug from her lips, a genuine smile slipping out this time at his misused word. "I'd like that."

As soon as Tommy left, Mrs. Steele joined Kara at the table. "How's your arm today? I can change the bandage after breakfast if you like."

Needing to get away as soon as possible, Kara slipped her arm into her lap beneath the table. "That's okay. It's fine."

Mrs. Steele gave her a motherly smile. "I imagine you'd like to call your family. You're welcome to use the phone."

"I'm a little old to be running to my mother with every little scrape," she said with a nervous laugh. Mrs. Steele patted her shoulder. "You're never too old for a mother's touch. Where do your folks live?"

"Back east," she responded automatically, then

focused on chewing her muffin. She and the deputy marshal had rehearsed her cover story dozens of times, but her mind was suddenly drawing a blank.

As if Mrs. Steele sensed how uncomfortable the questions had made her, she carried dishes to the sink and filled it with water. "You're welcome to stay here as long as you need to. Okay?"

Kara nodded, desperately trying to harden herself against the yearning to stay, to be with people who cared about her welfare. Clark certainly hadn't, and it'd been too many years since Mom and Dad had concerned themselves with what she was up to. Sure, she'd downplayed her need to go into hiding as a temporary measure, but they hadn't seemed particularly bothered by the prospect of not being able to contact her for an indefinite period of time.

Mrs. Steele returned to the table and patted her shoulder. "I washed your clothes. By the time Tommy puts Rusty through his paces for you, they should be dry."

"Thank you. I appreciate that. Then I can change for my morning run." This would be perfect. She'd have her own clothes and just wouldn't return from her run. Only, dare she put off leaving? How soon would Jake or his dad put in an appearance?

She resisted the urge to ask and instead quickly

finished her breakfast and joined Tommy in the backyard.

Outside, the weather hadn't improved much over the previous day, foggy and dreary, but at least it wasn't raining. Tommy handed her the dog's leash. "Hold him and count to twenty. Then tell him to find me."

Kara obliged, fondly remembering games of hide-and-seek with her own dog. When she silently reached twenty, she unleashed the dog. "Seek Tommy!"

Rusty bounded off, his nose to the ground like a hound dog. A few seconds later, Tommy squealed with delight at being found.

"You've done a good job training him to find you. Would you like me to show you a few other things you could teach him?"

"Oh, yeah. Daddy grumbles about him not listening. Can you teach me how to make him listen?"

Kara chuckled. "The most important thing is to be consistent with your commands and the hand signals you match to them, and then always expect him to obey." She showed Tommy the basic signals for sit, stay, heel and come. His eager questions and desire to try each one made her miss teaching her kindergarten children more than she wanted to. Despite how the situation had turned out, she'd done the right thing. She couldn't have lived with herself if she hadn't tried to save that child by going to the police.

The sound of a car engine slowing sent her into high alert. She peeked around the corner of the house. The car backfired and she nearly hit the dirt. A moment later, a teenage girl skipped out of the house across the street and got into the car, but that didn't slow Kara's racing heart. She needed to get out of here before Jake came back.

"Kara, phone for you," Mrs. Steele called from the back door.

Panic streaked through her. "Me?" No one was supposed to know she was here.

"It's Jake. He asked me to call him when you got up."

Oh. She took the phone, mentally trying to figure out a way to thank him and say goodbye without him realizing it was goodbye.

"Kara, I'm at your house. I'll be home soon to talk to you about what we've found. Okay?"

"Was it arson?"

"Yes, there's no doubt."

"Do they know who? I mean, was it like the other fires you mentioned? Do they think it could've been…?" Her voice trailed off. Why was she asking? The fire wasn't the work of some serial arsonist, even if whoever set it had tried to make it look that way. She knew it.

"Kara, do you have any enemies?"

And apparently Jake knew it, too. She swallowed hard.

"Kara?"

"No. What kind of question is that? I really appreciate your concern and help, Jake, but—"

Rusty spat out a ball at her feet and barked.

"I need to go." Kara tossed the ball to the other end of the yard. "I'm playing with Tommy and Rusty."

"Okay. But promise me you'll be there when I get back."

She stared at the phone, unable to get the lie past the lump in her throat. Finally, she hit End and whispered, "Bye," at the dead line. She left Tommy with a lame explanation, returned the phone to Mrs. Steele and fetched her still-damp clothes from the dryer before rushing upstairs to change.

She never should've pressed Jake with questions about the fire. All she'd succeeded in doing was make him suspicious. He was a good man. She hated to lie to him, but telling the truth wasn't an option.

Turning toward the bed, she startled at her reflection in the dresser mirror. She stepped closer, traced Jake's name embroidered on the left side of the jacket she wore. Had she imagined the appreciation she'd seen in his eyes as he'd surveyed her last night?

In another life, maybe he, instead of his mother, would have given her the jacket to wear.

No! She had no place for that thought. She yanked off the jacket, sending pain blazing down her arm in her rush. The heart flutters she got every time he looked at her were nothing more than a natural case of hero worship. He'd saved her life. Of course she'd find him attractive. Kind. Endearingly protective.

She glared at herself in the mirror. "Stop it." Hadn't Clark, let alone her father's fleeting concern, taught her anything? She didn't have time for such silly notions. Jake would be driving back from Hadyn any second, probably with the sheriff in tow, and she couldn't be here when he got back.

She pulled on her clothes and raced downstairs. "Mrs. Steele, thank you so much for everything. You've been so kind."

"Oh, dear, you say that as though you're leaving."

"No, no, just going for a run." She cringed at the telltale heat she felt creep up her neck. "I just wanted you to know how much I appreciate you giving me a place to stay and—" she motioned to her clean clothes, the muffins on the counter "—everything."

She let herself out the front door so she wouldn't have to face Tommy and Rusty again. Then, lifting the hoodie over her head, she turned north toward the highway and ran.

Jake found the sheriff on the sidewalk in front of what was left of Kara's house. "I need to get home. The marshal's going to give me a call once they clear an access to the cellar."

"Do you still think we're looking at the same guy who set the fires in your district?"

"From what I could see so far—" Jake buried his hands in his jacket pockets, not ready to float any other theories just yet "—yeah, I think so."

"I'm not so sure. I guess you heard about the gunman getting away last night?" At Jake's nod, the sheriff continued, "Makes me even more convinced that your first take on our victim was right. I don't think she's as innocent as she wants us to think."

"Because she happened to be in the same coffee shop?" Jake strained to keep his hammering heart from sounding in his voice.

"No, because we found her phone buried in the bathroom trash can. She'd pulled the battery. Clearly she didn't want us tracking her."

Jake's gut twisted at the memory of the panic he'd seen in her eyes. Didn't want the cops or the gunman tracking her?

He squinted at a guy sitting in a blue sedan

parked across the street, looking their way. "Hey, do you know that guy?"

The sheriff followed his gaze to the other side of the street. "No," he groused, but before he got two strides toward the car, the guy climbed out and headed their way.

"Excuse me. I'm looking for this woman." He held up a folded copy of that morning's Hadyn newspaper. A picture of Kara at last night's fire graced the right-hand quarter above the fold.

Jake fisted his hands, wishing he could strangle the byline-happy reporter who'd snapped the pic…right after he figured out whether this guy should be first in line.

"Do you know where I can find her?" The trench coat–clad guy asked, pushing shades he didn't need higher up his nose. "I understand she lived here."

"Who wants to know?"

"Oh, I'm sorry." He dug his wallet out of his back pocket and pulled out a business card. "Hal Walker, private investigator." He handed the sheriff his card and another to Jake.

The sheriff barely glanced at it. After all, anyone could print up a business card claiming to be anyone. "What's your interest in Miss Grant?"

"I believe she has information that may be of value to my client."

"Who's your client?" Jake interjected.

The P.I.'s gaze shifted to Jake, his head cocked. "Hey, aren't you the firefighter in the picture with her?"

"That's right."

"Do you know her?"

"Afraid not. Just met her at the scene last night. Who's your client?" Jake repeated.

"I'm sorry, that's confidential."

Jake bristled. Yeah, he could just imagine why. An irate ex-boyfriend or husband or whatever creep was after her, that she didn't want to admit to, wouldn't want his personal P.I. giving out his name.

"What kind of information are we talking?" the sheriff asked, clearly thinking he might dig up a motive for the fire.

"Information about pictures she took."

"When was that?" the sheriff pressed.

"A few months ago. So do you know where she's staying?"

The sheriff tipped back his cap as he scrutinized the guy. "Sorry, no."

"Was Sue living here when she took the pictures?" Jake fished.

The sheriff shot him a confused look, but the supposed P.I. didn't appear fazed by the bogus name. He shook his head and said, "No, she moved after that."

The reporter hadn't bothered to find out what

Kara's name was before going to print with his story. And apparently this P.I. wasn't surprised to hear her going by an alias...if he knew what her real name was in the first place.

Jake was beginning to wonder if *he* knew.

"Can I see other ID?" the sheriff asked as a hundred other questions Jake would like to ask raced through his mind.

The P.I. obliged by handing over a driver's license, and as the sheriff studied the card, the P.I. said, "Could you tell me where she works? Maybe I could—"

The sheriff gave him back his license. "Nope. Can't help you."

"Well, if you see her again, could you at least pass along my card? Tell her I'd like to talk to her."

Jake fingered the business card in his pocket. Yeah, Hal could count on it, but somehow Jake doubted she'd be interested in talking.

Kara's heart pounded as she neared the truck stop, and not from the sprint she'd taken to get there. She slowed her pace and surveyed the parking lot. The day Ray had brought her to Hadyn, he'd driven a tan Explorer. There wasn't one in sight. Her chest deflated. With Jake on his way home to talk to her, it was unlikely she'd get away with nursing a coffee at one of the tables all day until Ray showed up...*if* he showed up.

She skirted the vehicles and slipped in the side entrance. Burly looking guys filled the stools at the counter, and a few looked her way with an uncomfortably familiar glint of recognition in their eyes. She pulled her hood a little tighter and scanned the faces of the remaining patrons. Ray wasn't among them.

"Can I get you a coffee?" a waitress asked, holding up a pot.

"Uh, no, thanks. I was just—" Kara pointed toward the convenience store adjoined to the other end of the small restaurant and kept walking. If one of the guys back there was Ray's colleague, come in his stead, surely he'd follow her. Aside from a customer talking to the cashier at the checkout counter, the convenience store was empty. The customer wasn't Ray, but he seemed vaguely familiar. She came around the next aisle so she'd be able to see him from the front without drawing attention to herself. Only he turned her way at the exact wrong moment, their gazes colliding.

Her heart slammed into her ribs. Oh, no. She ducked her head and edged back down the aisle. It was Jake's brother. It had to be. She recognized his face from the photographs in the Steeles' home. And Mrs. Steele had told her he was a cop—ex-FBI, too. She pretended to be interested in the bottles in the back fridge, forced her breathing to slow.

What seemed like an eternity later, the bell over the door jingled his exit.

She closed the refrigerator door, almost collapsing against it in her relief. Except now she really couldn't hang around here waiting for Ray. As soon as Jake figured out she wasn't coming back, he'd likely enlist his brother's help to find her. An ex-FBI agent wasn't likely to forget a face like hers. Why couldn't God have given her an unmemorable oval-shaped face?

So what did she do now? Surely the bad guys would think she'd fled town by now, as any person with half a brain would have done. But if Ray had been compromised, this was the only place another marshal would know to look for her.

He'd specifically told her not to contact the marshal's office. But if she tried calling the number she had for him again, and the bad guys had gotten to him, with the right connections, they'd pinpoint her location in seconds. Unless…

She glanced out the store window. A trucker with California plates on his rig was filling up at the pump. If she borrowed his phone to make the call and he then headed south, the phone's pings off passing cell phone towers would lead the bad guys on a wild-goose chase.

She hurried out the door and was so busy keeping her eye on the trucker that she barreled into someone else.

"Whoa, there," he said in deep voice that sent a shiver down her spine. If his body hadn't been found floating in the river last week, she would've sworn the voice belonged to the creep she'd photographed selling that poor child.

"Excuse me. I'm sorry," she said, without making eye contact.

"Hey, you're the gal from the fire. How are you?"

She backed away. "Wh-what?" If this guy was from the marshal's office, she was supposed to ask, "Do you like fiddle music?" But—

He pulled out a newspaper he'd had tucked under his arm. "Your picture made the front page."

Oh. No. She felt the blood drain from her face. "Yes, I'm fine. Th-thank you for asking." She rushed toward the trucker. This couldn't be happening. If she didn't get hold of Ray fast, she wouldn't be able to show her face anywhere without being recognized.

A loud bark sounded behind her, followed by scampering feet and a chain rattling against the pavement. She shot a glance over her shoulder. No!

"Rusty, sit. Get over here." Jake's brother

stomped on the chain and Rusty came to an abrupt stop. "Sorry, he wouldn't hurt you. I don't know what's gotten into him," Jake's brother said without really looking at her as he wound the snapped chain around his hand. And thankfully, he didn't seem to notice the whimpering looks Rusty threw her way as he herded the poor dog through the parking lot. Any other day, she would've relished having Rusty join her for a run. But today she was on the run.

"Excuse me." She waved to the California trucker, who looked just about ready to pull the gas nozzle from his tank. "Um, I was wondering… Do you have a cell phone I could borrow for a quick call?"

He gave her a gap-toothed grin and pulled a phone from his hip. "Sure."

She gushed her thanks and then stepped a polite distance away as she tapped in Ray's number. Her heart leaped when he picked up on the second ring. "Ray, this is—"

"I'm sorry. I'm afraid Ray can't talk right now. He's been in a car accident."

Kara gasped. "Is he okay?"

"We're not sure yet. He's still in a coma."

A coma. "How…" She gulped. "How'd it happen?"

"The fog."

The fog? Not bad guys. Or was this one of the

bad guys trying to keep her talking long enough to figure out where she was calling from?

"Are you a friend?"

"Uh, yes. We were going to meet." She bit her lip. Should she have said that? She shouldn't have said that. But what if this was one of Ray's colleagues? Someone who could help her?

"I'm Ray's friend, Glen Rhoades. Perhaps I could help?"

"Uh, do you like fiddle music?" She held her breath, praying he knew the right answer.

"Sure…I guess." He drew out his response, clearly confused.

She hit End. "Only if a cat's playing it." That was what he was supposed to say, like the nursery rhyme. He could've just been a friend as he said, or…someone from the adoption ring. She shoved the phone back into the trucker's hand. "Thank you. I appreciate it."

She needed to get out of here before they tracked her down. But to where? She couldn't follow the highway.

Pulse racing, she turned back to the parking lot. Her gaze slammed into Rusty sitting fifty yards away. He sprang to his feet, tongue lolling, his rear end wagging a mile a minute. Jake's brother held his chain, leaning against the hood of his car, one foot on the bumper, arms crossed, watching the road.

She took off in the other direction. *Please, Lord, don't let Rusty try to chase me.* Behind her, a cell phone rang.

"Hey, miss," the trucker called after her, followed by the clank of the gas nozzle being returned to the pump. "Your friend wants to talk to you."

Pretending not to hear him, she picked up her pace. But she heard his response to the caller on the other end of the line. "At the truck stop between Hadyn and Stalwart."

The words fisted in her chest, squeezing the air from her lungs. *Oh, please, God, no.* Struggling to breathe, she stopped behind the cover of a semi. She braced her hands on her knees and gulped in air that didn't seem to get past the fear balling in her throat.

They'd...found...her.

SIX

Shielded by parked semis, Kara raked her fingers through her hair and turned in circles. *Lord, what do I do? I don't know what to do.* Gravel crunched behind her. She shot a glance over her shoulder and tensed at the sight of a dark sedan creeping toward her. She started walking in the opposite direction, but could feel the driver's gaze boring into her back. She tried to tell herself she was overreacting, that they couldn't have gotten here this quickly. But then why didn't the guy drive past?

The next instant, the car pulled beside her and her heart nearly pounded out of her chest. Slanting a glance at the car's heavily tinted windows, she quickened her strides. Two more truck lengths and she'd be in view of the gas pumps, the convenience store. Surely whoever was in the car wouldn't try anything in full view of a busy truck stop.

Suddenly the car swerved in front of her, the

door bursting open. She screamed as a glint of steel flashed over the hood and cold gray eyes speared her with a vicious gleam. "Time to say goodbye, Nicole."

At his brother's call, Jake swung by the truck stop on his way home. "Thanks for catching him," he said, reaching for Rusty's chain. "Tommy would've been dev—"

The dog bolted, yanking the chain from Jake's grip. Rusty sprinted past the shop, straight for the rows of parked semis. Jake raced after him with Sam on his heels.

"What is that dog's problem?" Sam shouted.

Rusty shot down one of the lanes.

"Stop!" Jake yelled, veering around the corner the dog had taken. He almost slammed into an empty car stopped in the middle of the lane.

A guy standing behind it shot him an angry glare, then jumped back in and swerved dangerously close to hitting Sam as he took off.

Ahead of them, the dog whimpered and army-crawled under a semi.

"Rusty?" Jake dropped to his hands and knees. "Are you okay, boy?"

"Jake?" Kara's voice rose timidly from under the truck.

One glimpse of her terrified face and Jake

reeled. The driver had been after her. "Sam, get that guy's license plate!"

Sam sprinted toward the far end of the parked semis, probably hoping to catch sight of the plate as the car swung onto the highway.

"Kara." Squatting, Jake extended his hand. "It's okay. He's gone." Except it wasn't okay. That guy looked like the gunman from the coffee shop.

She crept out on her belly, wincing every time she had to put her wounded arm down to pull herself forward. His stomach lurched at the sight of her scraped palms and torn pants and… He tilted his head and studied her eyes—one brown, one blue. "You lost a contact lens. Can you see okay without it?"

"What? I—" She scrambled to a sitting position, her expression morphing from confusion to panic as she clearly clued in to how he knew. She quickly popped the lens that remained. "Yeah, I can see okay." She ducked her head as Sam returned huffing.

Maybe the sheriff was right and she was up to her eyeballs in something illegal—so illegal she'd go as far as to change the color of her incredible blue eyes to not be recognized—but Jake wasn't willing to take the chance. Not when his gut told him she was innocent and needed help.

"I didn't get the plate. Are you okay, miss?"

Sam squatted in front of her next to Jake. "Did you know that guy? Did he mug you?"

"No, I'm fine. Thanks to Rusty." She hugged the dog and Jake had to tamp down a ridiculous pang of jealousy.

"You know the dog?" Sam slanted a questioning look in Jake's direction.

"She's staying at Mom and Dad's for a few days."

Sam cocked his head, clearly waiting for details.

"She's a friend," Jake said, afraid Sam would spook her with too many questions if he knew the whole story, or what little of it Jake knew. After what he just saw, the last thing he wanted to do was scare her into running off again. "Kara, this is my brother, Sam. He works with the sheriff's department."

"I'm sorry," she said. "I came out for a jog. Rusty must've followed me. I didn't realize."

Sam scratched the dog's head. "What I'd like is a description of the guy in the car and how he threatened you."

"Everything happened so fast. I—I just screamed, and then Rusty came and you guys and he took off."

"He was about five-eight. Shaved head. Pockmark on his left cheek," Jake filled in, then, glancing around to ensure the creep hadn't doubled back, quickly helped Kara to her feet. "C'mon, let's get you home." When she stiffened, as if she might object, he added in a tone that brooked no argument, "There are things you need to know before you do any more running." Her gulp told him she knew he hadn't bought her "out for a jog" story.

Sam gathered the dog's chain. "I'll need a name and address for the report."

"Do me a favor—" Jake took the chain from him, holding his gaze "—and make it an unidentified victim, okay?"

Sam's eyebrow arched a fraction of an inch, but he seemed to get the message. He'd been as angry as the rest of them when he'd heard how Jake's father-in-law had duped them. He knew all about how some things were better kept off the record.

"Sure, I'll try to get around tomorrow afternoon to help you and Dad finish the fence. Tying Rusty in the yard clearly isn't·going to cut it." He nudged Jake with his elbow and whispered for his ears only, "He's got good taste in women, though. I'll give him that."

Jake hid a grin, remembering how the dog had been glued to Kara's side all night. Apparently the dog wasn't as thick as he'd first thought.

With a sheltering arm around Kara's shoulders, Jake steered her toward his truck, then motioned her to climb in ahead of the dog. To the dog's credit, he nuzzled her into the center.

Jake chuckled, not about to make the dog move when his tactics ensured she wouldn't have an easy escape. "Rusty likes to sit by the window." He closed the passenger door and climbed in behind the steering wheel. She shifted toward the dog to give him more space, but her arm still pressed against his, sending a sensation dancing through his chest that he shouldn't be noticing.

His gaze skittered over the picture of his wife cuddling their newborn son. He fixed his attention on the road. If he was smart, he'd have let Kara hitch a ride with the next trucker heading out of town, or whatever other plan she'd concocted.

But he couldn't. Not after this. And not without, at least, warning her about the P.I. who'd been looking for her. Not to mention finding out everything she knows about their arsonist. Because clearly the arsonist knew her.

She shook her hair loose from her hoodie and a pleasant floral scent chased away the wet-dog smell hanging in the cab.

"Hmm, jasmine."

"Pardon me?"

Ouch, did he say that aloud? He shot her a sheepish look. "Your shampoo. Smells like jasmine. Much nicer than eau de dog."

A blush splashed her cheeks, and he couldn't

deny that he kind of liked being responsible for putting it there.

"Thank you for asking Sam to keep my name out of the report."

"You're welcome." Hopefully, it would be enough to convince her to trust him. He turned left onto the highway.

She gasped. "Where are you going? Your parents' place is the other way."

He monitored his rearview mirror and clicked up his right-turn signal. "I thought it'd be prudent to make sure we weren't being followed first."

She sank lower in her seat, her gaze shooting from one side mirror to the other. "Is someone following us?"

Jake made the turn and monitored his rearview mirror. "So far so good. Now, do you mind telling me who that guy back there was?"

"I don't know."

"Try again." Jake made another left. "I didn't get a good-enough look at last night's gunman, but I'm pretty sure this was the same guy."

She twisted in her seat and peeked over the back. "I wouldn't know. I never saw the gunman."

"But you thought he was after you."

"He stormed into the shop and yelled, 'Get down,' sounding as if he'd shoot them if they didn't. Who knows what a guy like that's gonna do?"

Jake gritted his teeth. What was it going to take for this woman to trust him? "You dumped your phone, and you expect me to believe you weren't afraid he was tracking you?"

Kara's shoulders drooped. Turning forward again, she sank even lower in the seat. "Is that your wife?" She pointed to the photo pinned to the dash.

"Yes." His voice edged higher. "She died because she didn't tell me how bad her situation really was. And if it's all the same to you, I'd just as soon not go through that again!"

She gaped at him, wide-eyed, as if he didn't already feel horrible enough for raising his voice. For blurting…

He scraped a hand over his face. "I'm sorry," he said softly. "Kara, I can see you're scared. I just want to help you."

"I guess if you know about the phone, you talked to the sheriff this morning."

"Yes."

Her leg jittered on the seat beside him, and he scarcely resisted the urge to still it with his hand. "Did you tell him I was staying at your parents'?"

Jake braked at the next corner and met her gaze. "No, Kara, I didn't."

"You didn't?" she repeated, sounding as if she didn't believe him.

He let out a ragged breath. After what he had

seen back there in the parking lot, he didn't think his assumptions were off base, despite her denials last night. He prayed that whether they were or weren't, she'd realize she could trust him. "Kara, my father-in-law was a cop, and abusive." Jake tucked a wayward strand of hair behind her ear, letting his thumb skim her mud-streaked jaw. "I understand not being able to trust the people you think you should be able to."

Moisture pooled in her eyes. Pure blue, intently searching his as if she might see into his very soul. If only she could, to see that he just wanted to keep her safe. She looked away, buried her fingers into Rusty's fur. "Thank you," she whispered, neither confirming nor denying his assumptions.

Lord, what am I supposed to do here? Jake wound his way through town, hoping she just needed time to open up. After another ten minutes of silence, he parked in his driveway next to his folks' house. "Kara, you need to know that your picture was on the front page of this morning's newspaper."

She stiffened, but remained mute.

"Who's looking for you?"

"What makes you think someone's—?"

"A P.I. came by your house this morning, looking for the woman in the picture. *You.*"

Her face turned ashen.

"Don't worry. I didn't tell him anything. Didn't trust him. He didn't even know your name."

She pushed past Rusty, reached for the door handle. "I can't stay here. You were in that picture, too. They'll—"

He caught her firmly by the shoulders. "Kara, listen to me." He forced her to turn and look at him as the dog whimpered at her distress. "They won't find you here. The only reason I was in that picture was because I'm the firefighter who helped you. The P.I.—if that's what he was—knows that. He's not going to come looking for you here."

She gulped repeatedly, her eyes round, looking as if she desperately wanted to believe what he was saying, but didn't. "I can't put your family at risk, Jake. I won't. I never sh—"

He gave her a hard shake. "Kara, I want to help you. But I can't do that if I don't know what we're up against. Who would hire a P.I. to hunt you down?"

She covered her mouth with her hand and shook her head.

"Kara, how can I help you?"

"You can't. I'm not sure anyone can."

SEVEN

"Do you believe in God?" Jake asked.

Kara hesitated, her hand still on the door handle of his truck, the dog nudging her arm to be let out. Did Jake? Her mind whirred through reasons why he'd ask.

A car rumbled past the driveway and she jerked at the sound. Her limbs trembled uncontrollably. The gunman's words—*time to say goodbye, Nicole*—replayed in her mind. The instant she'd seen the gun, she'd thought it was the end. She hadn't even had time to pray. Then, like a blur, Rusty had come out of nowhere. Then Jake.

As much as it felt, with all these bad things happening, that God didn't care, He'd kept her safe through each incident.

"Kara?" Jake touched her hand.

She blinked. Met his penetrating gaze. "Yes. Yes I do believe in God."

The corners of his lips tipped up a fraction. "Then let's pray, because I know *He* can help you." Jake's warm fingers folded over hers before she could choke out an answer, so she simply bowed her head and hoped he'd do the praying, because her heart was pounding so hard she didn't think she'd be able to hear her own words.

His deep voice resonated through her. "Lord, we thank You that You are sovereign. We thank You that it is not Your will that anyone should perish. We don't know the heart of this man who's threatening Kara, but You do. Please, change his heart." Jake's thumb stroked a gentle rhythm over her fingertips, stilling her trembling. "Please protect Kara and show her what she should do. And show me how I can help her."

He didn't open his eyes or say "Amen" and, in the silence, a peace crept over her.

Then Rusty let out a woof that sent her practically jumping into Jake's lap.

Tommy yanked open the door. "You found him!" Rusty leaped out of the truck and smothered him in kisses.

"Sorry about that," Jake said as he let Kara out his door. She couldn't help the trembling that had returned with a vengeance at Rusty's bark or the heat that flamed her cheeks when Jake consolingly squeezed her hand. She'd been just about ready to confide in him, but maybe God had brought Tommy to the truck at that very moment for a reason.

Over and over again, the marshal had reiterated how important it was that she not tell anyone she was in witness security. Except, if whoever answered his phone could be believed, Deputy Marshal Ray Boyd couldn't help her anymore. He wasn't going to show up at the truck stop. And even if his partner knew of their fail-safe site to meet, she didn't dare go back there now. If the guy behind the adoption ring could tap a marshal's phone and get his goon onto her that quickly, he clearly had more powerful connections than even the marshal had anticipated.

Another car rumbled by on the street, and Jake herded her toward his parents' side door, his body shielding her from view of the road. "C'mon, sport," he called over his shoulder to Tommy. "I'm sure Gran has lunch about ready."

Kara breathed a relieved sigh at the sight of leftover turkey, ham and sandwich fixings spread on the table. Jake wouldn't pursue his questions in front of Tommy and his parents, and the reprieve would give her time to figure out what to do. "Oh, this looks wonderful, Mrs. Steele. Let me just get cleaned up and I'll be right back."

Jake stepped in front of the stairs, blocking her escape. "After lunch, we need to finish our conversation, okay?"

She tilted back her head to meet his gaze. He was a lot taller than she'd realized, at least a couple of inches over six feet. And to anyone else, with the way his muscular arms and shoulders strained at his fire department T-shirt, he probably looked downright intimidating, but she couldn't shake the image of those strong arms cuddling his sleeping son last night, or the warmth of his touch as he'd prayed for her. Deep down, she knew that he wouldn't force her to tell him anything she wasn't ready to, even as frustrated as he clearly was with her reticence.

She nodded and raced upstairs, leaving him to field his mother's questions about the tear in her slacks and the dog's escape.

As she quickly scrubbed her hands, she reviewed her options. She didn't dare try dialing the marshal's number again. If the bad guys hadn't actually caused Ray's accident, at the very least they had to be tapping his phone, or else how would they have found her at the truck stop so soon after her call? And returning to the truck stop was out, which meant she'd have to break one of the marshal's cardinal rules, because now that she'd thrown away her phone, and her house was uninhabitable, the marshal's office had absolutely no idea where to find her, unless she initiated contact. That had to be safer than confiding in Jake. After all, how could Jake really help her, except to give her a place to hide for a couple of days?

She couldn't stay in hiding forever. And now that the bad guys knew she hadn't left the area, as a sane person would have done, they'd be combing every back alley for her.

Except…what about this P.I. Jake mentioned? Had the adoption ring hired him, too?

It didn't make sense when they'd already found her. When they'd already burned down her house! Unless they figured they didn't want their own guys asking the police questions. Yeah, that had to be it, because otherwise the police would be able to identify them later when she turned up dead.

Her insides lurched. Water splashed on her sleeves and chest. She snapped off the tap, clutched the edge of the sink. *Lord, I can't do this alone. Please.* Slowly, the infernal shaking eased. She drew a deep breath, then another. *Please, Lord, connect me with a marshal who can get me out of here.*

She dried her hands and peeled off her now-damp hoodie. As she tossed it into the bedroom she'd used last night, she scanned the dresser top and night table for a phone. None. The doors to the other upstairs rooms were closed, and she didn't feel right about snooping around for a phone, especially when everyone might be waiting for her downstairs. No, she'd make the call after lunch. She was pretty sure she'd seen a cordless phone in the kitchen. She could take it into the bathroom to make the call, where she wouldn't be overheard.

As she returned to the kitchen, Mr. Steele set a plate on the counter and stole a kiss from his wife. Her heart kicked longingly at the sight. In all her growing-up years, she'd never seen her dad playfully steal a kiss. She remembered the day Clark did. They were unpacking a picnic lunch she'd made, and his spontaneous show of affection had made something shift inside her. She'd let herself start thinking that maybe he was different from other men—men like her father, who only cared about their careers. She should've known better. If there'd been one good thing about her becoming entangled in this whole adoption ring nightmare, it was that it let her see Clark's true colors before she made a fateful mistake.

"Look, Miss Kara, I spelled your name," Tommy shouted gleefully from the table, where he sat with his dad arranging plastic letters into words. "K-aaa-rrr-aaa," he sounded out.

"Wow! That's very good, Tommy."

Jake's gaze lifted to hers with a fatherly pride that made her heart flutter. How differently might she have thought of herself if she'd ever seen that look in her own father's eyes? Jake was a good man.

Tommy peered up at her, his forehead wrinkling. "Hey, your eyes turned blue like mine and Daddy's."

"Wow, you're observant," she said, with as upbeat a tone as she could muster with Mr. Steele looking to Jake, one eyebrow cocked and Mrs. Steele stealing a peek at her eyes. "I was wearing colored contacts before," she explained. "I thought it might be a fun change for a while."

"Cool."

Kara shifted her attention to the letters on the table and slipped into the seat on Tommy's other side. "What else can you spell?"

Tommy quickly rearranged the letters. "Mommy. My mommy's in heaven. Right, Dad?"

Jake gave his son a sideways hug and kissed the top of his head. "That's right." His voice cracked. "But she loves you very much."

"And she doesn't want me to be sad that she can't be here," Tommy said matter-of-factly, as if this was a subject they'd discussed many times.

Unlike his dad, Tommy didn't seem upset by the loss, and Kara wondered how long ago his mother had died. She couldn't help but admire how hard Jake clearly worked to ensure his son knew how much his mother had loved him.

Mr. Steele prayed for the meal and steered the discussion toward happier subjects. He and his wife shared snippets of the Alaskan cruise they'd taken that past summer to celebrate their fortieth wedding anniversary, and laughed at how Jake's brother had fallen in love with the woman he'd been on the cruise to gather evidence against.

"Really?" Kara sneaked a glance at Jake. When he'd asked Sam to keep her name out of the report, she'd sensed more was being said than what was spoken. Had Jake won his brother's acquiescence by letting him believe he had feelings for her?

"She was innocent." Jake popped his last bit of sandwich in his mouth and winked. "The Lord brings people together in mysterious ways."

Jake's wink, or maybe the intimation in his tone, unleashed a flurry of butterflies in Kara's middle that she needed to ignore. He couldn't have meant what it sounded as though he meant, as if maybe the Lord had brought *them* together.

She was overwrought, sleep deprived, practically out of her mind with panic not knowing what to do. He'd just been talking about his brother. Or maybe, just implying she should accept his help, considering how God kept allowing him to come to her rescue. Yeah, that had to be it. Because he was clearly not over his wife.

Not that it would matter, because she would be leaving soon. Very soon. As soon as she got hold of the marshal's office.

Eyeing the phone, she pushed her chair back

from the table. But at the same moment, the side door burst open and Sam strode in.

"Uncle Sam," Tommy squealed and catapulted into his uncle's arms.

"What are you doing here?" Jake said. "I thought we were going to work on the fence tomorrow." Jake stiffened and Kara tracked his gaze to the newspaper tucked under Sam's arm.

Oh. No.

"Goody! Can I help?" Tommy shouted.

Sam set the boy down. "In a little while. Maybe Miss Grant can read you a few books while your dad and I take care of the hard stuff first."

Kara's blood turned to ice at his use of her last name—a name that neither she nor Jake had mentioned at the truck stop. A name that according to Jake hadn't been in the paper either. Which meant Sam—former FBI agent Sam—had been doing his homework.

"Do you mind?" Jake looked at her apologetically, and it took her a couple of seconds to clue in to his request.

But how much had Sam discovered? What was he here to do? Why did he want to talk to Jake and not her? Or more important, why did he want to talk to Jake *without* her?

EIGHT

"I'll be out in a second." Jake pushed Sam outside with his dad as his mother cleared the kitchen table. He hadn't missed the way Kara had tensed the instant she'd spotted the newspaper in Sam's hand. And he had a bad feeling any trust he'd gained during their conversation in the truck would be lost the longer he stood outside talking to his cop brother. Jake hovered at the doorway to the living room, where Kara and Tommy had settled into the recliner.

She didn't look as if she'd bolt before he returned. Aside from Sam's fiancée, he'd never met a woman who interacted with his son so naturally and who Tommy had taken to so unreservedly. Even the dog was smitten. Rusty snuggled up against the chair and laid his head on the armrest, nuzzling her arm until she scratched his neck.

The sun glistened through the window, creating a halo effect around them that would've made a stunning picture. His mind drifted back to their shared prayer in the truck. He'd felt ten feet tall when he'd taken her hand in his and her trembling had finally eased. If they'd had a few more undisturbed moments, he was certain she would have confided in him.

Tommy held up his *Are You My Mother?* book, and Jake's heart clenched.

His son was growing too attached to a woman who he was pretty sure didn't plan on sticking around. Jake fingered the P.I.'s business card and wondered for the hundredth time if he'd been an idiot to invite her here at all.

The kind of jerk who came after a fleeing woman wouldn't think twice about collateral damage. Except…since Sam had clearly figured out that Kara wasn't *just* a houseguest, maybe he would run a background check on the P.I. for him, see if the guy was even legit. A P.I. with any kind of morals wouldn't help an attacker locate his prey. He might even disclose his client's name once informed of why the guy really wanted to find her.

Yeah, maybe Sam finding out who Kara was wasn't such a bad thing after all.

Jake quietly backed away from the doorway, and, ignoring the glint in his mother's eye, slipped outside.

Sam dropped the pile of fence poles he'd been moving and wasted no time getting to the point.

He snagged the newspaper from his back pocket and slapped it into Jake's hand. "Why didn't you tell me she was the arson victim?"

"It didn't seem relevant."

Sam's eyeballs actually bulged. "Excuse me? Yesterday someone burns down her house, and today someone tries to grab her, and you don't think they're connected?"

Dad's gaze bobbed from Sam to Jake. "Someone tried to grab her? Was it the gunman from the coffee shop?"

"What? She's connected to that, too?" Sam shot Dad a flabbergasted look. "You knew someone was after her and you let her sleep under your roof?"

"Of course." Dad crossed his arms, straightening to his full height, which put him eyeball to eyeball with Sam. "It was probably the safest place for her to be."

"Safe for her, maybe," Sam said through gritted teeth. "Until this creep tracks her here. Then none of you will be safe."

Dad let out an indignant snort and snapped the tape measure to the last fence post they'd erected. "I was a cop for over forty years." He marked the spot for the next hole. "I'm not about to let an irate ex-boyfriend, or whatever he is, scare me out of helping a woman in need."

Sam planted his hands on his hips and glared

at Jake. "Is that who you told him was after her? An abusive boyfriend?"

Jake plowed his hands through his hair. "I don't know who's after her. That was my guess, because last night when I found her running from someone in the hospital parking lot, she had the same look April's mother had when her husband threatened her."

"Okay, wait a minute." Sam tamped the air as if that would cool everyone's rising tempers. "You're telling me you've seen this guy before?"

Jake shrugged. "I didn't get a look at the guy in the hospital parking lot. But yeah, the guy I saw this afternoon looked like he could've been the gunman from the coffee shop last night."

"And you didn't think you needed to tell me that?"

"Shh." Dad patted the air this time, darting glances to the neighbors' yards.

"The guy shanked two of our deputies," Sam hissed.

Jake blew out a breath. "I know. But my father-in-law was a cop, too. Remember?" He clenched the newspaper in his fist. "And Kara seems petrified of the police knowing where she is, so I figured that if I had any hope of winning her trust, I needed to help her stay below the radar."

"Below the radar?" Sam's voice shot up again.

"For all you know, you're aiding and abetting a criminal!"

"She's not a criminal," Jake said firmly.

"Definitely not," Dad agreed. "I've seen all kinds over the years. Kara's not one."

Sam picked up the auger and drove it into the dirt with anger-charged jerks. "I can't believe you condoned him not even telling the sheriff where she was."

Jake's heart slammed into his ribs. He grabbed Sam's shoulder. "You didn't tell him, did you?"

"Of course not." Sam yanked free of Jake's hold and jabbed a finger into his shoulder. "But you need to."

Jake pulled the P.I.'s business card from his pocket. "Can you do me a favor, first, and find out who this guy is and why he wants to find Kara?"

Sam scanned the card. "A P.I.? Where'd you get this?"

"Or so he claims." Jake told him the guy's story as Sam jotted down the contact information, then added, "I think Kara might be ready to tell me what's really going on. At least she seemed to be, until you showed up. She'd agreed to talk after lunch."

Sam glanced at the house, then went back to auguring. "What do you know already?"

"At the fire, she kept saying she had to get to the coffee shop to meet a friend. But when I found her after the gunman had shown up, she didn't seem to have a friend in the world. I know she's petrified of someone finding her. Whether he's her so-called friend, I don't know. But she even dumped her cell phone for fear he could use it to track her."

Dad grimaced. "She was probably right."

"Shoot, why didn't I think—" Jake pulled out his cell phone and dialed the sheriff's number. "Hey, Sheriff, it's Jake Steele."

Before Jake could ask his question, the sheriff launched into a full description of what they'd found in the cellar of Kara's house. "The fire marshal says that both the type of string used as a trailer and the brand of candles were different from in the other four fires. Those details were never reported in the news, which makes him confident we're dealing with a copycat."

Which meant not only did Kara have a sicko after her, there was another sicko out there, likely planning his next arson for inside of a week, if he kept to the same schedule. "Let's hope this copycat's stab at the limelight hasn't ticked our first guy off, or chances are his next fire will be scarier than ever."

"Yeah, the fire marshal said the same thing. This fire's looking more and more like an effort to bilk the insurance company, and I'm not convinced that our missing victim didn't have a hand in it."

Seeing his opening, Jake jumped in with the reason he'd called in the first place. "Did you happen to check Kara's phone? Find out who she called last night?"

"Yeah, and that's what has me even more suspicious of her. She called the same number four times. Unfortunately, we can't get an ID on who it belongs to. But the first call went out only minutes before the 9-1-1 call for the fire. And one was a text message that said, 'I'm at the coffee shop. Where are you?'"

Jake restrained a groan. With two deputies injured by the gunman, it was no wonder the sheriff had his sights set on a woman who'd been waiting for someone at the same coffee shop. And if he knew Jake was keeping her whereabouts from him…Tommy could be visiting his dad in jail.

He had to convince Kara to come clean with what was really going on, or he'd have no choice but to turn her in.

"I found out where she works from her landlady," the sheriff went on. "Her boss had no qualms sharing her schedule with us, so I should have her in custody by Monday morning. I appreciate your help on this. You may want to check in with the fire marshal, but I don't think this particular fire investigation will be of any more interest to you."

Right. If he only knew.

Kara let the curtain slip back into place as Tommy and Rusty bounded out the door. If the rigidness in Jake's posture was anything to go by, he hadn't been happy with whatever Sam had to say. But more worrisome was the sight of him on the phone as he'd crushed her picture in his fist.

Mrs. Steele headed upstairs with a laundry basket and Kara snatched up the kitchen's cordless phone. She locked herself in the main floor bathroom, and then realized she didn't know the number or know where the Steeles kept a phone book, and the landline didn't have the option of going on the internet to check.

The slap of the screen door rattled the windows. Great, someone was coming inside. Now what?

She could call the operator for the number, but then she wouldn't be able to block her number from being seen.

"Kara?" Jake's voice drifted through the door.

"Uh, I'll be a few minutes," she called and could hear his mother say something to him, but couldn't make out the words. Terrific—paper-thin walls. At least the washroom door was at the end of the hall, not exactly a convenient place for him to hover while he waited.

She dialed zero and, in as quiet a voice as she could use and still be heard, asked the operator to connect her to the marshal's office in Seattle. "Yes, hello, may I speak with Deputy Marshal Ray Boyd, please?"

"I'm sorry, he's unavailable."

So whoever answered his phone yesterday might not have been lying. Kara tightened her grip on the phone. "Is there another way I can reach him? It's very important."

"Were you talking to me?" Jake asked through the door, causing Kara to miss whatever the receptionist said in response.

"Uh—" Kara covered the mouthpiece with her hand "—no, I was just talking to myself. I…um… could be a few minutes."

When she heard the sound of his footsteps fade, she pulled a towel over her head, uncovered the mouthpiece and whispered, "I'm sorry. Could you repeat that?"

"Hello, this is Deputy Marshal Peter Towns," a male voice responded. "How may I help you?"

"I need to talk to Ray Boyd."

"I'm afraid he's had a medical emergency and will be out of the office for an indefinite time."

"Did— Was—" Her heart pounded so hard she couldn't form a coherent question. "What happened?"

"A traffic accident."

"You're sure? It was an accident, I mean?"

"Who am I speaking with?"

Kara's heart ratcheted up another gazillion beats a second. "Uh, who will be handling Ray's cases?"

"I am, ma'am. If you'd give me your name, I'd be happy to answer any other questions I'm able to."

"Ray was supposed to meet me last night," she said without giving her name. "He was going to get me out of here."

"Out of Stalwart?"

Her breath caught in her throat. He knew where she was. She wrestled in a breath. Of course he knew. She didn't block the phone number. But if this guy was handling Ray's cases, she needed to tell him where she was anyway.

"Ma'am? What's your name? Why was Ray coming to get you?"

"They torched my house." Her fingers clenched the phone so tight, the plastic cracked. "I don't know what to do."

"Who torched your house?"

"How did they find me? He said they wouldn't find me. I didn't break any rules."

"You're right," he soothed in the same tone she'd use on a child in the throes of a temper tantrum. "This isn't your fault. I'm afraid some of our cell phones were recently compromised."

"Compromised?" She pressed the towel to her mouth and forced her voice down an octave. "What do you mean *compromised?*"

"Someone hacked into the phones. We discovered the breach about an hour ago."

"Breach? You mean someone's listening in on this call, right now?"

"No, I assure you this line is secure. If you'll give me your name and location, I will personally come get you."

Didn't he already know where she was? He'd mentioned Stalwart. Except for all she knew, *he* was the hacker, and he'd just said all that to win her trust.

Outside, it sounded as if someone was leaving. She glanced out the window and spotted Sam heading toward the driveway. What if he told the wrong cop about her? The leaked story in the Boston paper had proved that they couldn't all be trusted to keep her safe. Maybe none of them could. They just wanted to catch their criminals.

She was nothing more than a means to an end.

"Ma'am, are you okay? Is someone threatening you right now?"

Her breath came in short gasps. She leaned

back against the wall and slid to the floor. "Do you like fiddle music?" she blurted, suddenly remembering the code phrase Ray had given her to vet imposters.

"Sure, doesn't everyone?"

She clicked off the phone, pressed it to her pounding chest. If he'd truly been Ray's partner, he'd have said, "Only if a cat's playing it." *Oh, God, what have I done? He didn't know. He didn't know what he was supposed to say.* And she'd been on the line so long, he'd probably traced her call or reverse looked up the number or whatever bad guys did.

He knew where she was!

A loud knock startled her into dropping the phone. "Kara? Are you okay?"

"Yes." Only her voice sounded anything but, as she scrambled to grab the phone that had slid across the floor. Standing, she set it on the counter, pressed a towel over top of it so he wouldn't know until after she left that she'd been on it. Except…she couldn't leave without warning him that someone bad might come here looking for her. Might not believe them when they told him she wasn't here.

Or he could be a deputy marshal as he'd said, someone she could trust. The operator had made the connection after all.

How do I know, Lord?

"Kara?" Serious concern laced Jake's voice.

She straightened her hair, drew a deep breath and then opened the door. "Sorry I took so long. I thought there was another bathroo—" Her words faltered at the intense disappointment in his gaze.

"Did you get hold of your friend?" he asked quietly.

"My—?"

"I know you were on the phone, Kara. It's not a crime. I wouldn't even expect you to ask to use it. But don't lie to me, okay?" He turned away, strode to the living room.

Dragging her feet, she trailed after him. "You're right. I was trying to call my friend. I shouldn't have. I'm sorry."

He pivoted on his heel and closed the distance between them, clasped her upper arms. "You don't have to apologize for needing to talk to a friend." His touch, his words grounded her spiraling fears.

She squeezed her eyes shut, unable to face the compassion blazing in his. "You don't understand. Someone else answered. I don't know if he can be trusted. And I didn't block your parents' number. He'll know where I am. He'll come—" She choked on the thought. "I need to go."

Jake tugged her against his chest and folded her in his arms. He rested his cheek against the top of her head. "It's okay." His whiskers rasped against her hair as his rumbly voice reverberated through her. He tightened his hold, and the steady beat of his heart against her ear momentarily blocked the warnings screaming through her mind. "Kara, my dad was a cop for forty years. His number is unlisted. Whoever answered your friend's phone isn't going to track you through it, not without some sophisticated hardware to trace the call."

"The operator must have told him. He knew I was in Stalwart."

"Just from the exchange. He's not going to get the address."

She swallowed the panic that had balled in her throat. "Really?"

"Really." He relaxed his hold and, gripping her shoulders, put an arm's-length distance between them and waited until she met his gaze. "You're safe here."

She blinked back the tears that pressed at her eyes. "I wish I could believe that."

Jake guided her to the sofa and urged her to sit, then pulled over a side chair. The graze of his knees against hers filled her with a comfort she didn't deserve. Not when she'd endangered his family by foolishly using their phone. "Kara, as I'm sure you figured out by his sudden appearance, Sam knows who you are."

"He does?" Her voice squeaked. Jake's mom had said Sam only recently moved from Boston.

She should've known that seeing her picture in this morning's paper would tweak his memory of her appearance in the Boston papers.

"He thinks we should talk to the sheriff."

"The sheriff?" she repeated dumbly.

"Yes, before this gets any worse for you."

"I don't understand."

"The sheriff thinks you're connected to the fire, and to the gunman in the coffee shop, and not in an innocent-victim kind of way."

She pressed a hand to her burning chest. "He thinks I'm a criminal? But you said Sam—" She pursed her lips. Apparently his brother didn't know who she *really* was.

"Sam hasn't said anything to anyone, because he didn't want the family to get in trouble for harboring a fugitive."

"But I'm not a fugitive!"

"Your disappearance and that P.I.'s asking after you have the sheriff suspecting otherwise. He learned where you work and intends to take you into custody the next time you show up."

Good thing she didn't plan to return, then.

Jake reached for her hand. "If you tell me what's going on, who you're afraid of, I think together we can convince the sheriff that you're the victim here, not to mention have a better chance of helping him stop the guy. That's what you want, isn't it?"

"Of course, but…" She stared at Jake's large, strong hand dwarfing hers.

"I know you're worried that somehow this guy will hear that you snitched and track you through whatever deputies you talk to. Believe me, I understand. But what other options are there?" He squeezed her hand. "I don't want the creep I saw after you today to ever get a chance to get that close again."

Kara closed her eyes, absorbing the comfort of Jake's fierce protectiveness for just a moment. Her reticence must make no sense to him at all. And truthfully, it was beginning to feel pretty fruitless to her, too. Except she could see now that while hunkered down in the bathroom, trying not to be overheard, she'd overreacted to the deputy marshal's wrong response to her coded question. She hadn't even given him her name. And he obviously hadn't realized the significance of the question.

"Do you think the guy who found you today is the same one who hired the P.I.?" Jake asked, jolting her from her thoughts. He did genuinely seem to care what happened to her. She supposed that kind of caring was in the genes of a firefighter like him, and not really personal, but that didn't stop her heart from somersaulting at his gentle persistence.

"I imagine so, yes."

Sam stormed into the room and Jake shot back in his chair, dropping her hand as if it was on fire.

She tried not to let that hurt as he sprang to his feet.

Sam held up a cell phone and wiggled it. "We need to go."

"Go where?" Jake snatched the phone. "And what are you doing with my phone?"

"You left it in your jacket. Davis called from the station. Some guy came in looking for you. Said if you can't come talk to him, he'll come to you." Sam slanted an and-you-don't-want-him-coming-here look in Kara's direction.

"Right." Jake touched Kara's hand to regain her attention. "Promise me you'll stay put until we get back."

Her heart stuttered at the concern in his vivid blue eyes. But how could she make such a promise? Sam clearly thought this guy was looking for her and, if he had so much as an inkling that Sam or Jake might know where she was, he'd follow them right back here.

NINE

Davis intercepted Jake and Sam outside the fire station before they got out of Sam's car. "He's in the back room. Says he's a deputy marshal."

Jake exchanged a vehement look with Sam and fitted on his ball cap. A federal marshal. If this was about Kara, it was shaping into a sickeningly familiar scenario. "Did he say what he wanted?"

"No. You in some kind of trouble?"

Jake slammed his car door. "Not that I know of."

As Sam joined them, Davis added, "The guy's kind of shifty. That's why I didn't want to give out your home address. I'm not even working today, just dropped by to pick up my coat. Figured I'd stick around until you got here."

Jake nodded. "Appreciate it."

"Did he show you a badge?" Sam asked.

"Oh, yeah. Not that I'd know a real one from a fake one these days. If you know what I mean."

Jake strode through the open bay door and,

as Davis veered off to one of the trucks, Jake slanted a glance at Sam. "How do you want to handle this?"

"Just ask him what he wants. I'll hang back and try to read his reactions as best I can."

Catching a glimpse of the burly guy through the window that looked into the truck bay, Jake swiped his suddenly sweaty palms on the legs of his jeans. The guy had a good eighty pounds on him and, from the look of the bulge under his gray blazer, he was packing heat.

Jake entered the small break room and, extending his hand, rounded the table dominating the middle of the room. "Jake Steele." He hitched his thumb over his shoulder. "And my brother, Deputy Sheriff Sam Steele. You wanted to see me?"

The guy clasped Jake's hand in a weak grip, his gaze flicking to Sam. "Deputy Marshal Clay Rogers."

Sam remained near the door and, crossing his arms, leaned back with his shoulders and one foot braced casually against the wall.

"How can I help you, Deputy Marshal?" Jake asked.

"I'm looking for Kara Grant. I was told that you might know where she is."

Jake frowned. "The victim I found at last night's fire? Why would anyone think I'd know where she is?"

The marshal's eyes narrowed. "The paramedic who drove her to the hospital said you took a special interest in her."

Gritting his teeth against a few choice words for his too-talkative cousin, Jake willed himself not to break eye contact. He couldn't believe Sherri would be so stupid.

"His partner—your cousin, I understand— didn't think so."

Jake mentally apologized for blaming Sherri as the marshal presented a printout of the online version of the front page of Hadyn's morning paper.

"But the two of you do look cozy in this picture."

Jake snorted. "I never met Miss Grant before last night. She turned toward me because she didn't want the reporter snapping her picture. That's all."

The man nodded, his perusal uncomfortably intense. The air in the too-small room seemed to grow scarcer by the second as the marshal took his sweet time refolding the paper and inserting it into his blazer's inside pocket. "You haven't seen her since you put her in the ambulance?"

Jack backed up a step, bumped into a chair. He glanced at his brother. If he outright lied, the marshal was bound to read some giveaway tell in his face. His brother always could. He shook his head. "When I saw deputies swarming the coffee shop that she'd mentioned needing to get to, I stopped to see what was going on. They'd taken down a gunman, but she was gone." Satisfied with his evasion, Jake crossed his arms and searched the marshal's face for any telltale signs he had a connection to the gunman. At half a foot taller and half a ton heftier, he couldn't be mistaken for the gunman, but that didn't mean he hadn't hired the hood to pick Kara up, or worse.

"A guy came after her in the coffee shop?"

Jake shrugged. "I thought it was just a robbery." He tipped back his ball cap and, scratching his head, threw his brother a help-me-out-here glare.

Sam pushed off the wall. "Why are you looking for her? Is she in some kind of trouble?"

"Nothing you need to concern yourself with." The deputy marshal swaggered toward the door. "Sorry to have taken up your time."

The instant the marshal stepped into the truck bay, Sam whipped out his cell phone and scrolled through screens.

"That was the best you could do?" Jake muttered, and edged closer to the window overlooking the bay to see if the guy stopped to question anyone else on his way out. He supposed he should be grateful Sam wasn't laying into him for withholding information from a federal agent, considering. "What are you doing?"

"Trying to find out if this guy is who he says he is."

"You think he's an imposter?"

"I don't know. He was cagey."

"Yeah, kind of reminds me of my father-in-law. Don't you think?"

Sam glanced past Jake then strode to the small window facing the side street. "Yeah, you might be right."

Jake's insides burned with the sudden compulsion to stalk after the guy and plant a fist in his face.

Sam pointed out the window. "Looks as if he's waiting for us to leave."

"What?" Jake lurched across the room, sending a couple of chairs flying from his path. The guy sat in a black Marquis, his attention fixed on the fire station. "You think he didn't believe me?"

Sam pocketed his phone. "Not sure. He probably has no other leads and figures following you home will confirm this one, one way or the other."

Jake's pulse skyrocketed. "We can't let that happen."

"See if Davis is still here."

Davis appeared at the door. "Did I hear my name?"

"Yeah." Sam snatched Jake's ball cap off his head and told him to take off his jacket. "Want to go for a ride with me?"

Davis arched an eyebrow.

Sam jutted his chin toward the window. "Lead the marshal on a wild-goose chase."

Davis laughed. "Love to."

"Good." He handed him Jake's cap and jacket. "Put these on. Can Jake borrow your car?"

Davis dug out his keys and tossed them to Jake. "Baby her."

"What am I supposed to do with his car?" Jake asked.

"Wait until you're sure the marshal's following us in the opposite direction, then get yourself home and find out from that woman what's really going on."

Jake grinned. "Good plan. I'll park the car at Davis's sister's and jog the rest of the way. That way you won't have to bring him back to the house to get his car."

Davis agreed and pulled down the ball cap. "How do I look?"

Sam chuckled. "Just keep your back to his car and the marshal won't know the difference. Jake, give us a good five minutes before you leave. I'll call if he veers off before then."

"Got it." Jake's fingers tightened around the keys as he prayed Kara stuck around that long.

Jake turned up his shirt collar against the misty chill as he jogged the last three blocks to his parents' house. The glow of a computer screen seeped past the slanted blinds of Dad's office. The rhythmic ping of a sledgehammer slamming metal traveled from the vicinity of the backyard. Jake slowed to a walk as he reached the driveway. If his dad was still working on the fence, hopefully the light in the den meant Kara was still here.

He joined his dad in the backyard. "Where is everyone?"

"Your mom took Tommy to the Black Friday sale to get that new action figure he's been after. Your friend is in my den, if she didn't sneak out the front while I wasn't looking. You learn anything I should know?"

"Not yet. But pray I can convince her to trust me, okay? Because I've got a real bad feeling about where she's heading if she doesn't let someone in."

Dad squeezed Jake's shoulder. "Lord, give Jake the words that will convince Kara to trust him, to trust You, to know that we sincerely want to help her, to help her stay safe." Dad's hold tightened and his voice grew wobbly. "Our lives are in Your hands. We know that. But—" His words faltered and Jake hugged him, struggling to shut out the memories rising like a specter to taunt him.

"Thanks, Dad. Keep praying."

"I will, son."

As Jake turned toward the back door, he glimpsed movement at the kitchen window. His heart did a funny staccato in his chest. Had Kara seen him standing in the middle of the yard, praying with his dad?

He pushed through the door and she sidestepped away from the window, her arms folded over her chest, looking very much as if the last thing she wanted to do was talk.

"Hey." He gave her a lopsided smile. "Thanks for staying."

Her arms tightened around her middle as she shrugged. "Had nowhere else to go."

The light glistened off a single tear clinging to her impossibly long eyelashes, and his heart cracked open.

"Where's Sam?"

"Leading the guy who was looking for you out of town."

Her face turned ashen, making her eyes look even bluer, more frightened, more desperately alone. "Who?" she choked out.

Jake shepherded her into the living room and urged her to sit. He flicked on the switch for the natural-gas fireplace to take the chill out of the room and then sat in the chair he'd pulled close earlier. "He said he was a deputy marshal. Clay Rogers. Do you know him?"

She shook her head, but from the bob of her

throat and the whiter her cheeks paled, he didn't believe her.

"Kara, why would a deputy marshal want to speak to you?"

She averted her attention to the box of Christmas decorations his mom had left on the coffee table. "Does your family put up a real Christmas tree? I always wanted—"

"Kara?"

She picked up a strand of silvery garland and twisted it nervously. "Are you sure he was a marshal?"

"No, but Sam will find out for sure."

"Why—" Her voice faltered; she chewed on her bottom lip. "Why didn't you tell him where I was?"

Jake reached for her hands. They were like ice. He pried the garland from her hands and rubbed them between his own. "A guy tried to kill you, Kara. I'm not about to tell anyone where to find you. I don't care if he claims to be the president of the United States."

A tiny smile quirked the corners of her lips, sparking a flicker of hope that she'd finally open up to him.

"Kara, I want to help you if I can. But I can't protect you if I don't know who I'm supposed to be protecting you from."

Her gaze dropped to their clasped hands, and

his heart did a traitorous jig. His instant reaction was to jerk away. How could he hold this woman's hand so...so intimately, here in the same room where he'd once courted his wife?

But something deep inside him stayed the reaction. If he was going to convince Kara she could trust him, she needed to see that nothing would make him turn away. Not even the oppressive sense that he was a hypocrite. If he'd been half as determined not to accept April's pat answers five years ago, she might be alive today. His eyes blurred.

"It's not your job to protect me," Kara whispered, not looking up.

He eased one hand from hers and lifted her chin until she met his gaze. "Everything in me says otherwise."

Kara's heart melted at Jake's words, at the warmth of his touch. No one had ever felt compelled to be there for her before. Certainly not Clark. Her father hadn't even been there to celebrate her accomplishments. He'd even missed her high school graduation.

She recalled the sight of Jake's dad squeezing his shoulder a few moments ago, of them bowing their heads together in prayer, their hug. Yearning tightened her chest.

She gave her head a mental shake. She should

be grateful that, as absent as he'd been, at least her father had provided for their physical needs. That was more than a lot of people in this world could say. Besides, the Lord was a father to the fatherless.

The tightness in her chest intensified. These past couple of days even God had felt absent.

Her gaze skittered over the Bible on the side table, the Bible verse plaque propped on the mantel above the fireplace, Jake's hands cradling hers just as they'd done when he prayed with her earlier. No, God wasn't absent. He'd brought her to this place of refuge. Maybe even to a man she could…

Her heart thundering, she lifted her gaze to Jake's. "Why do you care what happens to me?"

He blinked, clearly caught off guard by her question. His lips pressed together as if he might not answer.

At the apology in his eyes, her insides twisted. Why had she asked? No man would ever care for her *that* way. And she certainly never intended to pin her hopes for happiness on a man anyway. That was one lesson her parents had taught her well. She tried to ease her hands from his hold.

Jake held them fast. "I don't want another woman to die on my watch."

She stilled. "You're talking about your wife."

A heavy sigh deflated Jake's chest. "My wife

died because I didn't pay enough attention to what was going on."

Kara squirmed at the admission that made him sound uncomfortably like her absent father.

"My mother-in-law died at the hands of her abusive husband two months before Tommy was due. My wife took it really hard and went into early labor because of it. Because I failed to convince her mom to press charges in time to save them."

"It's not your fault," she whispered.

He rubbed his knuckles over the vicinity of his heart. "Tommy was born healthy and that helped ease April's grief, but she was really tired, even after days in bed. I was concerned, thought we should go back to the hospital. But it was Thanksgiving and my turn to work. She said it wouldn't be fair if I called in, said she'd be fine, so I asked my mom to stay with her." He shook his head, his eyes unfocused. "April didn't tell me how heavily she was still hemorrhaging. Clots we learned later from not moving around enough. But I should've recognized the signs. I shouldn't have gone off to work. I—"

Kara pressed her fingers to his lips. "I'm sorry for your loss." Her heart ached at the anguish on his face. He'd obviously cared deeply for his wife.

He clasped her fingers, drew her hand back down to her lap. "Please let me help you, Kara.

You have a P.I. and a federal marshal and a gunman after you, not to mention the sheriff. How much longer do you think you can stay ahead of them on your own?"

She should've trusted Peter Towns. Whether or not he was familiar with Ray's cases, he, at least, was a marshal. He'd said he'd come personally to get her. Except...some other guy claiming to be a deputy marshal had shown up at the fire station. Within twenty minutes of her call! Had he sent him, or did their phone breach go a lot deeper than they knew? If she'd told him her location over the phone, the wrong guys could have beaten Peter here.

Concern radiated from Jake's gaze. After all he'd said and done, she was sure she could trust him, and right now she didn't know who else she could trust. And he was right. With so many people looking for her, left to her own devices, she wouldn't get far before *someone* found her.

She pushed to her feet. "Let me show you something." She marched to his father's den and opened the computer's web browser. A few clicks more and the image of the body pulled from the Charles River appeared on the screen.

Jake sank into the office chair and scanned the article beneath the photograph. His brow furrowed. "This happened two days ago on the other side of the country. What does it have to do with you?"

She'd been searching the internet for this story, hoping the discovery of a dead adoption agency employee would expedite the arrests, but aside from a vague reference to the kindergarten teacher who'd raised concerns about illegal adoptions happening in Boston, the article was mute on the investigation.

She pointed to *kindergarten teacher* on the screen. "That was me."

His eyes widened.

"My real name is Nicole," she rushed on. "Until three months ago, I lived in Boston."

Something akin to pain darkened his eyes.

She looked away, needing to say it all before she lost her nerve. "I was jogging with my dog in the park and when I stopped to tie my shoe, I overheard two men talking on the other side of some bushes. From the snippets I caught, I was certain they were up to something illegal. So I snapped photos of them with my cell phone."

Staring at the body on the computer screen, she rubbed her arms, but couldn't dispel the chill that crept through her bones or the chilling thought that she was next. "When money and a child exchanged hands, I realized I'd stumbled upon a black market adoption, or worse. But before I could get away, they heard me."

She tore her gaze from the image and paced the room. She paused at the bookshelf, at the photograph of Jake's wife holding her newborn son—the same photo he had in his truck. He had a son. Unlike Clark, he'd at least understand why she'd had to go to the police with the photos. She cleared her throat. "One guy—" She pointed to the small employee picture superimposed over the corner of the image of the dead body. "That guy pulled a gun and ran after me. I managed to get away. I went to my boyfriend's work. Told him what happened. He told me to go home, to forget about it. He told me that I didn't want to get messed up in anything like that, that organized crime was behind things like that and that I'd be dead by morning if I went to the police. He actually got mad at me for coming to his work with my dog as if he was afraid I'd led them to his doorstep." She swiped at a tear, furious that his reaction still hurt so much.

Fisting her hands, she turned to the window. "I went to the police with the photos and begged them to rescue the child. They'd supposedly been trying for some time to crack a black market adoption ring operating in town. But instead of arresting the men in the photos, they decided to keep them under surveillance, or at least the one they could identify, hoping he'd lead them to the real brains behind the operation."

"What about the child?" Jake said vehemently, clearly thinking about his own son.

"They said they needed to consider the future children they'd be saving, that they'd eventually find this boy, too."

Jake scraped his hand over his mouth, shaking his head.

"They told me not to talk to anyone about what I saw. But the next morning a reporter broke the story on the front page of a Boston newspaper—Kindergarten Teacher Exposes an Alleged Black Market Adoption Ring, the headline said, accompanied by a grainy picture he must've snapped of me as I left the police station."

"What did the police do?"

"Nothing at first. I didn't even know about the article until one of the teachers at school was reading the paper at lunch break. She pointed to the photo and said, 'Hey, that's you.' I tried calling the officer I'd talked to, but was only able to leave a message." She watched Rusty prance around Jake's dad in the yard, the pain swelling in her chest. "When I got home that same afternoon, there was a package waiting for me. I—" She choked at the memory. Struggled to stuff back down the pent-up sorrow clambering for release.

Jake stepped up behind her at the window, turned her into his arms. He didn't say anything, just held her, and the warmth of his unspoken support melted the ice around her heart.

"It was a bomb," she blubbered between sobs. "My—my sweet pup tore into the package. His mischievousness saved my life. But I lost him."

Jake stroked her hair. "I'm so sorry, Kara."

She rushed on to keep from falling apart completely. "The police put me in the witness security program. Shipped me out here. Told me I couldn't tell anyone who I really was. And I didn't. I didn't. But they still found me."

Jake's arms tightened around her. "It's going to be okay."

And in his protective arms, she could almost believe it. Almost. She pushed her palms against his chest. "I wasn't supposed to tell you."

He cradled her face in his hands, capturing her gaze, his own resolute. "It's going to be okay," he repeated, emphasizing every word.

She pulled his hands from her face, and injected a strong dose of resolve into her backbone. "The friend I tried to call was the marshal who's supposed to get me out, but they told me he'd been in a car accident. But what if it wasn't a car accident? What if this guy hurts you, too? You have Tommy to think about." At the flick of a muscle in his jaw, her voice faltered. "Maybe I should've just let that marshal come get me, except…I didn't know if I could trust him."

"Deputy Marshal Clay Rogers?"

"No, he said his name was Peter Towns. And he said he'd come get me *personally*. So there's a good chance that the guy at the fire station was a bad guy."

"Sam will be able to figure out that much," Jake murmured.

"No!" Kara clasped Jake's arms. "You can't tell Sam what I've told you. I wasn't supposed to tell anyone."

Jake's tender look communicated how much he appreciated her gift of trust. "He can help us connect you to a marshal you can trust."

She shook her head. "The more people who know…" She drew in a sharp breath. "Wait. My handler's true partner would know where I worked. He might ask for me there."

"Let's call your boss, then, and find out." Jake handed her the phone.

She tapped in star sixty-seven first to ensure the number wouldn't show on her boss's caller ID. Never mind that Jake didn't think it could be traced back to the house. "Hi, this is Kara," she said when her boss answered. "I'm afraid I won't be able to come to work for a few days. My house—"

He expressed his sympathy for her situation.

"You know?" Of course, he must've recognized her picture from the newspaper.

"Yes, the sheriff called and a couple of other fellows, too, trying to find out if I knew how to contact you."

Kara turned to Jake, the blood turning to ice in her veins. "Two men asked about me?" She hadn't even realized she'd clutched Jake's hand until his thumb swept across her wrist, sending a surge of reassuring warmth through her body. She took down the information and then relayed it to Jake. "One man called only an hour ago. Didn't leave a name."

"Could've been the marshal I spoke to."

She handed him the paper she'd written the other man's name on. "This guy called this morning. Asked my boss to ask me to call him."

Jake pulled a business card from his back pocket and compared the names. "That's the supposed P.I. who stopped by your house this morning."

Her legs wobbled. She braced her hands on the desk. "The adoption ring leader must've hired him to find me."

Jake nudged her into a chair, then whipped the office chair around and, taking a seat, pulled himself up to the computer again. "I asked Sam to see what he could find out about him, but then we got called to the fire station. Let's see what we can learn from the internet." He typed in the guy's name and a slew of sites came up confirming his affiliation with several private investigation associations. Jake typed in an image search next. "Well, that's the guy. So he is a P.I."

Kara picked up the business card Jake had placed on the desk. "Do you think he'd tell me who he's working for?"

"You can't call him. That's too dangerous. Sam could get a female deputy to call and impersonate you." He scrubbed his hand down his face, muffling a groan. "Except even that is risky. She'd need to tell him that she got his number from your boss, not me. We don't want this P.I. to deduce that I'm helping you and track you to here."

The sound of scurrying feet and clicking dog nails sounded in the kitchen, headed their way.

Kara swallowed her objection to involving Sam. "Okay, we'll do it your way," she said, a second before Tommy skidded into the den, holding up a superhero action figure.

"Dad, look what I got! It's just like Lucas's."

Jake swooped Tommy onto his lap and took a commendable interest in the gadget, considering the slant of their conversation only moments earlier. Rusty planted himself in front of Kara, obviously expecting some attention of his own.

"Hey, how'd you get him to do that?" Jake said.

"Do what?"

"Sit to be petted, instead of jumping up."

She chuckled. "I don't pet him until he sits. Positive Reinforcement 101," she added with a wink.

"Gran and I saw another goldendoodle just like Rusty outside the mall," Tommy blurted. "I petted-ed him. And a man drove up in a black car and asked if his name was Rusty."

Kara exchanged a panicked look with Jake. "You didn't tell him *you* had a goldendoodle named Rusty, did you?"

Tommy shrank against Jake's chest at her abruptness. "No, Gran said we had to go."

"That's good," Kara responded more softly this time. "Because you should never talk to strangers. You know that right?"

"Yeah, that's what our teacher says."

Jake bounced the knee Tommy sat on. "You don't tell them your name or about your family or pets or even mention houseguests like Kara. Do you understand?"

"No." He thumbed the toy in his hands. "But I don't talk about that stuff anyway."

Jake pressed a kiss to the top of his head. "That's good. Why don't you go see if Gran has some milk and cookies for you?"

"Yay." Tommy bounded off Jake's lap. "You want some, Miss Kara?"

"No, thanks, Tommy. I'm not hungry." What little food she'd eaten at lunchtime churned in her gut. "That had to be the man from the truck stop," she hissed the instant Tommy scooted out of the room. "He's prowling the town looking for the dog. To find me! What if it had been Tommy and Rusty, not some other owner's dog he happened upon? What if he checks with local breeders to track Rusty down?"

"My dad got Rusty through a cop friend. He's not going to tell some stranger who he sold his dogs to."

"Jake, this man torched my house, came after me with a gun. He's not the kind of guy who takes no for an answer."

TEN

At the sound of Rusty barking outside, Jake tore his gaze from the blazing fire in Kara's eyes and burst out of the den. "Tommy, call the dog inside and keep him in."

Jake's mom intercepted Jake in the hallway. "Tommy's playing upstairs. The dog's fine. Your father's still out there."

"No, Mom, he needs to stay in the house." Jake slipped past her to the back door and whistled. Once Rusty was safely inside, Jake turned to his mom. "That guy you saw in the mall parking lot, asking about the goldendoodle, what did he look like?"

Mom's eyes widened and strayed to the wall that separated them from Kara waiting for him in the den. "Is he who's after Kara?"

"It's possible."

"I knew he was slippery when he asked if the dog's name was Rusty." She fussed with the tea towel in her hands.

Fear flamed in Jake's chest at how close the creep had been to his boy, at what might've happened if Tommy had blurted that *his* dog was called Rusty. "Can you describe him, Mom?"

"Yes, he wore a black leather bomber jacket. Had a shaved head. Was shorter than Sam. Maybe five-eight. Oh, and he had some sort of tattoo on his arm. When he petted the dog, the base of it peeked out the bottom of his sleeve."

He sounded like Kara's attacker, all right. "Can you find me the number of Dad's friend who sold you Rusty?"

"Yes, I have it right here." She reached into the catchall drawer next to the fridge and pulled out an address book. "Did Kara confide in you? Tell you why he's after her?"

Jake's grip tightened on the address book as his conversation with Kara replayed in his thoughts—the vulnerability in her voice when she'd asked why he cared what happened to her. He could still feel the heat on his lips where her touch had branded him as she'd stopped his explanation, apology in her eyes. He cringed at the thought that it had been easier to admit to his failure as a husband than examine his motives for protecting her too closely.

He tried not to think about how perfectly she fit in his arms or notice the lingering fragrance of her shampoo on his shirt. Any man would have offered a comforting hug to still her trembling. It didn't mean he felt anything more than concern for her. And even if he did, it wasn't as if it mattered. She was in witness security. As soon as they connected her with a marshal they could trust, she'd move on and he'd probably never hear from her again.

It might not be her choice, but the choice wouldn't be hers to make.

"Jake?"

He jerked his attention back to his mother. "Just keep Rusty inside, okay?" As Jake headed back to the den, he thumbed the breeder's number into his phone and made short work of ensuring he, at least, wouldn't give Kara's attacker a lead on their place. At the sight of her sitting at the desk, tapping a number into the phone, his heart rioted. "Who are you calling?"

Squinting at the computer screen, she tapped faster.

He stormed across the room, saw the website for U.S. Marshals and hit Disconnect.

She hooked her fingers into the base of the phone and pulled it out of his reach. "I need to call them, Jake. I can't endanger your family any longer." The tiny indentation at the base of her throat convulsed, belying the steel thread propping up her voice.

"But you said yourself that you didn't know if

you could trust them. The supposed marshal who came to the fire station didn't look like a guy I'd want to trust your protection to. He had a handshake as limp as a rotten banana."

"I overreacted before. You were hovering outside the bathroom door. I wasn't thinking straight. Now I am. Clearly this is my only option."

He backed toward the wall, planning to pull the cord from the phone jack if she refused to listen to reason. "Let's talk to Sam first, okay? He's ex-FBI. He can ensure you connect with a marshal you can trust." Jake's chest tightened. What if the next marshal didn't do any better a job than the last one at keeping her safe?

Kara twisted the phone's receiver in her grip. "The marshal's office would be furious with me if they found out I confided in him. They might refuse to acknowledge me, even."

Jake glanced at the contact information on the computer screen and fought the fleeting suspicion that she'd made up the whole witness security story and was afraid Sam would out her. His mother-in-law had been uncannily creative at spinning stories to explain her bruises. Jake's fingers curled into his palm as his mind replayed Kara's story. She was terrified the gunman would find her, no matter who'd hired him. He had no doubts about that. But maybe, like his mother-in-law, she wasn't afraid enough to risk anyone else getting caught in the middle.

"The marshal's office can hardly blame *you* for confiding in someone." Jake softened his voice. "They're the ones who screwed up by leaving you exposed like this."

The rambunctious sounds of Tommy and Rusty playing sounded over their heads.

Kara tugged her bottom lip between her teeth, her gaze straying to the ceiling.

Jake snapped the phone cord from the wall jack and closed the distance between them. "Kara, he's not going to find you here."

"You don't know that." Her eyes darkened to midnight-blue, a shade of determination he couldn't help but admire as much as he hated to see it. "I went to the police with those photos to save a little boy's life. I won't risk another boy's to save mine."

"Tommy isn't in danger." Jake's cell phone rang and he snatched it from his hip. "It's Sam," he said as he clicked it on.

"Turns out Deputy Marshal Clay Rogers is legit," Sam said, the sound of a squad room in the background. "Did Kara tell you why he'd be interested in her?"

"Yeah."

"Are we looking at another loose cannon like your father-in-law?"

Jake held Kara's uneasy gaze, pouring all the reassurance he could into his own. "Can you come here?"

"Sure. I lost Rogers's tail, but do I need to switch vehicles in case he's trolling the streets looking for my car?"

"That'd be good."

Ten minutes later Sam pulled into the driveway in his fiancée's Ford Focus. He paused briefly in the backyard and chatted with Dad, who was still working on the fence, then came inside.

A moment later he appeared at the den door with a tray. "Mom made coffee."

Jake relieved him of the tray and made a mental note to give his mom a big hug later. He'd been a bear avoiding her earlier questions. They each took a cup and a seat, and at Kara's request, Jake recounted her story to Sam.

"The Happy Family Adoption Agency?" Sam's focus turned to Kara.

She nodded. "I guess you saw the picture of the dead employee they fished out of the Charles River yesterday?"

Sam's brow furrowed. "No, I just heard a report on the radio about a sting operation in Boston, resulting in a handful of arrests."

"Really?" Kara straightened, a hopeful glint in her eyes. "If they've arrested them on more evidence, then the case won't hinge on my testimony anymore. I'll be able to go home!"

Sam moved to the computer and ran a search on the name of the adoption agency. "They arrested the owner for selling babies to the highest bidder. He apparently coerced desperate young mothers to falsify birth certificates."

"Will the biological parents get their children back?" Kara asked.

Sam shook his head. "It could prove difficult. Client records were destroyed before the police moved in. Any adoptions that bypassed ordinary registration channels will be near impossible to track."

Kara visibly deflated. "It's not fair."

"Not for either side. The article claims several clients of the agency contacted police to ask if the adoptions of their children were legal. They claim they had no idea the agency wasn't operating legally. Could you imagine having to give up a child you'd raised for years?"

Jake moaned. "It would rip me apart."

"But the child deserves to know his birth parents." Kara squirmed. "To know that maybe they hadn't wanted to give him up."

"Not arguing with you," Sam interjected. "Just saying it's going to be emotionally devastating all the way around. But what matters right now is finding out if the arrests mean you'll no longer be targeted. Let me make a few calls."

As Sam stepped out of the room, Kara's gaze sought Jake's. "If the adoption agency hired the gunman, surely he won't bother me now. My testimony will hardly matter."

Jake shifted closer and squeezed her hand. "That's assuming he's heard the news. In any case, the police will still want to catch him. He has a lot of charges to answer to."

"Chances are good the P.I. will tell us who hired him now that the adoption agency's been exposed. Don't you think?"

Jake blew out a breath, quickly skimming the online article himself. "I guess it depends on who he's more afraid of. The law or the thugs."

Sam returned, looking grim. "The owner of the adoption agency denies hiring anyone to silence Kara."

"Of course he does," Jake growled. "That doesn't mean he didn't."

The taut edge to Sam's jaw told him that the danger to Kara was far from over. "You believe him?"

"My friend on the Boston P.D. claims the guy is spilling his guts in the hope of gaining a reduced sentence."

"I don't doubt it, but he's got to know that admitting to conspiracy to commit murder would put him away for good." Jake winced at the shiver that trembled through Kara at his mention of murder.

"Have they tied the employee's death to anyone?" she squeaked.

"No. It has all the markings of a mob hit, but the agency owner swears he's never worked with organized crime. Claims he was as surprised and horrified by his employee's death as anyone."

Kara frowned. "They said the bomb at my house in Boston had looked like a mob hit, too." Her knuckles whitened as she shakily returned her coffee mug to the tray. "I guess the police will want me to stay in hiding awhile longer?"

The sadness in her voice wrenched at Jake's heart. She was a stronger person than him. Losing his wife had ripped a hole through his life. But he could scarcely imagine having been able to find his way through without the support of family and friends, whereas Kara had had every support ripped out from under her, save God alone.

"Yeah, they will." Sam shot Jake an indecipherable look. "My friend on the Boston P.D. is contacting the Seattle marshal's office now. He'll let them know what's going on and find me a trustworthy contact. Then we'll arrange for you to return to their protection."

Jake sprang to his feet and paced, feeling like a caged animal—powerless. "What are the police doing to find this guy?" The sheriff's deputies hadn't landed a single lead from interviewing Kara's neighbors. And aside from maybe tracking down where the string and candles were purchased, the evidence they'd scrounged did little more than offer fodder to a profiler.

"We have a BOLO out for the guy and his car. After what he did to two of our own outside the coffee shop, you can be sure every deputy between here and Seattle has eyes peeled for him."

Kara reached for the business card on the desk. "Couldn't you pressure this P.I. to tell you who hired him?"

"Yeah." Jake agreed. "Or follow him? Or something?"

"Actually, the adoption ring didn't hire him," Sam said. "A couple whose child was kidnapped did. My friend in the Boston P.D. told me the P.I. has harangued him a number of times. Wanted to see the photos Nicole—" Sam motioned to Kara "—uh, you brought in."

"Really?" She reached for the phone. "I need to talk to him, then. If the child I saw was theirs—" Her forehead furrowed and she looked oddly at the phone receiver. "The phone's dead." She gulped, her gaze darting to the window.

"It's okay," Jake soothed. "I unplugged it."

Sam took the phone from her hands. "It's probably better if you wait until the marshal gets here."

"No, he won't let me talk to the P.I. I know he won't."

"If that's true," Jake jumped in, "then it's only to ensure your protection."

"But what if I saw something that can help this couple find their child? Can you imagine the agony they must be in?"

"Yes, Kara, I can." Jake sank to the seat beside her and reached for her hand. "But—"

She jerked away. "My boyfriend thought I was crazy to go to the police with those pictures, but I knew that I couldn't sleep at night knowing I might have been able to do something to save that child and reunite him with his parents."

Recalling the nightmare his mom had mentioned Kara having last night, Jake wondered if it still haunted her.

"I need to talk to him and at least give those poor parents what answers I can." Her eyes pleaded with him to understand.

Jake exchanged a look with Sam, who didn't look any more eager to approve the call.

"What if this were Tommy?" Kara pressed. "You'd be on my tail until I answered your questions. You know you would. Besides, in a way, I'll be safer if I talk to him now, because then there'll be one less person trying to track me down and maybe exposing my location."

Yeah, but exposing her location was exactly what he feared.

Kara's insides quivered as the next day, she and Jake approached the picnic area his brother had chosen as a meet site. "I thought Sam said the place would be deserted."

A dilapidated van sat in the corner of the parking lot, and she counted at least three people in the park.

"They're the deputies watching your back," Jake whispered. "Sam filled the sheriff in just enough to get you off his most-wanted list and secure protection. He said there'd be a lady with a stroller."

"I see her. Over by the fountain." Kara lifted her hand, but Jake immediately grabbed it. And the playful warmth with which he held it captive sent a whole different kind of quivering through her middle. Jake was so different from any man she'd ever known—a man who might make her forget all the reasons she shouldn't get involved in a serious relationship. Her gaze drifted back to the baby stroller and a lump lodged in her throat. She probably should be relieved that she was about to be whisked out of town and wouldn't have time to explore this unexpected attraction.

Jake released her hand and stopped to tie his shoe. "The jogger on the track circling the playground is another one of Sam's men."

Feeling too much like a target standing in the empty parking lot in the bright red coat she'd borrowed from Jake's mother, Kara pulled the hood's string tighter. The fur edging tickled her nose, but at least the coat did a better job of shielding her face and camouflaging her body shape than the hoodie the bad guy had seen her in yesterday morning at the truck stop.

Was it really only yesterday? It seemed like an eternity ago.

Jake stood and jutted his chin toward a guy walking a terrier. "That must be the third deputy over there."

Kara reached underneath her coat and tugged at the very uncomfortable Kevlar vest Sam had insisted she wear. Jake's father had dropped them off two blocks from the park, but between the vest and the coat, she'd worked up quite a sweat on the drive—a sweat that now dripped annoyingly down the center of her back, making her feel itchy where she couldn't reach to scratch. "What are we supposed to do now?"

"Look like a happy couple out for an afternoon stroll." Jake captured her hand again, his calloused palm rasping against hers as he brought it to his lips. His deep blue eyes darkened as their gazes met over their joined hands and the lingering effect of his ever-so-soft lips.

He's playing a part, she reminded herself. But her body wasn't listening. Delicious tingles traveled up her arm and swirled in her chest. "It's the stress of the situation," she muttered.

"Pardon me?" Jake slowly lowered her hand, his gaze still holding her captive.

Heat rose to her cheeks that had nothing to do with her heavy coat. "Oh, I, uh, was just wondering when the P.I. would get here."

Jake blinked as if he'd momentarily forgotten why they were there, as if he hadn't been playing a part at all, and her heart did a swirl of its own. He steered her toward the track. "Shouldn't be long. To be on the safe side, Sam asked the P.I. to meet him at the police station and then planned to slip him out the back door to bring him here, just in case anyone tapped the P.I.'s phone or followed him."

Kara hid a smile as they walked the track the opposite direction to the jogger. Sam had had to do a lot of fast talking to convince Jake that he could still keep her safe when she'd adamantly refused a meeting at the police station. She wouldn't be surprised to learn that Sam also sent a lookalike of her out the front of the police station to lure away any waiting bad guys.

Jake nodded to the jogger as he passed them,

then searched the grassy knolls surrounding the park. He tightened his hold on her hand, his expression as gray as the sky. "Are you sure you want to do this here? Now? There's still time to change your mind."

"Yes, Jake. If I can help this couple find their son, it will make everything I've been through worth it."

His thumb stroked the back of her hand soothingly. "You're an amazing woman. I can't imagine how lonely and frightening these past few months must have been for you."

Unused to words of praise, she squirmed, even as his soft declaration nestled into a lonely corner of her heart. "Not so amazing. I've been feeling pretty frustrated and impatient at how long the police were taking to make the arrests."

"That's understandable."

In the front yard of a house across the street from the park, a father and child strung lights around a manger scene.

Kara let out a wistful sigh. "One good thing about all that's happened, I suppose, is that I've spent a lot more time talking to God." She snickered. "Even started listening to His answers."

"Yeah, know that feeling." Jake's clasp tightened as he quickened their pace around the track. "After my wife died, it took me a lot of sleepless nights before I finally knew He was there, realized that He'd been there all along. His ways still made no sense to me, but I knew with certainty that He loved my wife more than I ever could."

"Yes." Kara choked on the word, utterly humbled by the sweet love that still resonated through his words whenever he talked about his wife.

Jake cleared his throat. "So what's God been telling you?"

"Oh." Kara shrugged off her woolgathering and focused on Jake's question. "I guess, like you experienced, mostly assuring me that He's near, even when it doesn't feel like it. I've been reading a lot of David's psalms."

"Have a favorite?"

"Yeah. 'If I settle on the far side of the sea, even there your hand will guide me, your right hand will hold me fast.' And, 'Even the darkness will not be dark to you, the night will shine like the day, for darkness is as light to you.'"

Jake nodded. "I've recalled that verse a time or two when struggling to find victims in a smoky house."

Kara marveled at how easily Jake talked about leaning on the Lord. In the six months she dated Clark, she couldn't recall ever having a spiritual discussion with him. He joined her for church every Sunday, and okay, once or twice they'd talked afterward about the sermon, but... Maybe it was as Jake said, that sometimes it took a lot of sleepless nights to truly *meet* God. To have Him become the first person you turn to in a crisis instead of the last.

Jake tucked her arm beneath his. "They're here," he whispered so softly it took her a moment to decipher what he'd said.

A green Ford Escort parked under the arching boughs of a giant oak tree with a few indomitable leaves still clinging to its branches. Kara drew a deep breath, willing the same resolute spirit into her own shaking limbs. Sam emerged from the driver's side and a squat man with dark hair and a square face, wearing a trench coat, as cliché as a Sam Spade movie, climbed out the passenger side.

Jake glanced down the road and around the park's perimeter then escorted her to the same picnic table that Sam and the P.I. headed toward. Sam's equally furtive glances around the perimeter made her steps falter. The P.I. seemed to have no such qualms. He eagerly reached across the table and shook her hand. "Thank you for agreeing to meet with me."

"I'm not sure I can help your clients, but I'll try."

"That's all I ask." He opened a file folder and pushed a photograph of a tawny-haired boy of maybe four or five months across the picnic table. "Is this the boy you saw in the park in Boston?"

"I couldn't say. I scarcely saw the boy. He was bundled in a blanket. Didn't the police show you the pictures?" Hopelessness swept over her like a tidal wave, its undercurrent threatening to yank her feet out from under her. *Lord, please don't let this be in vain.*

"This blanket?" The P.I. pushed another photograph across the table as Sam ambled around them, making her insides tremble all the more.

She stared at the face of a smiling infant teetering on a mint-green, hand-knitted blanket, her heart breaking. "No, I'm sorry. It was yellow fleece."

As if sensing her despair, Jake eased the photo from her hand. "You have nothing to be sorry for."

The P.I. changed tactics. "What do you remember about the man who took the child?"

"Didn't you see the pictures I took?" She wrung her hands. How had she thought she could help?

"Yes, but none showed his face or anything that would help us ID him. I'm hoping you might remember something that will."

Jake covered her hands, urging them to still. "Close your eyes and picture the scene. Tell us everything you see."

She closed her eyes. Could smell the damp

earth, hear the babble of the water over the rocks. "It had rained that morning. Everything was wet." She remembered thinking how out of place the two well-dressed men had looked standing around a picnic table at the river. Her heart quickened at the realization that she could picture him as if he were standing right in front of her. She'd knelt to tie her shoe, to afford a longer look. The one had lifted his foot onto the table as he leaned forward over his knee for a closer look at the child. "He wore polished black leather shoes, expensive looking. Not what I expected to see on a guy in the park."

"That's good. What else?" Jake urged.

She squeezed her eyes tighter, saw the man edge the blanket back from the child's face. "He had a ring on his pinkie. A chunky one with a big topaz stone."

"Could be his birthstone in a school ring," Sam suggested from behind her as the P.I. scratched notes on his pad of paper.

"Right or left hand?" he asked.

She held up her hands, mentally positioning the two men in her mind. "His right."

"What about distinguishing marks? Scars, moles, a tattoo?"

She shook her head. "Not that I noticed."

Jake squeezed her hand. "How about vehicles? Did you see what the guy drove?"

Kara closed her eyes again and mentally scanned the scene. "Yes. Maybe. There was a fancy silver car parked not far away. The woman in the passenger seat was watching the two men."

"Can you describe her?"

"No, not really."

"How about the car? Do you know what kind it was?"

Kara let out a frustrated sigh. "Sorry, I'm not good with cars." It had frustrated Clark to no end that she had no interest in them. Maybe she should've been paying more attention when he had been expounding on the merits of each while trying to decide which one to buy.

"Did it have a hood ornament or decal?" Sam asked, now standing behind the P.I.

"Yeah." She squinted, trying to bring the image into focus in her mind. "It had three circles on a diagonal on its front air filter thingy."

"On the grille?" Jake clarified.

"Yes. Do you know what make that is?"

Sam flicked through images on his cell phone and held out one labeled Audi for her to look at. "Are you sure it wasn't four rings like this?"

"No. The circles were kind of pointy and definitely on a diagonal."

Jake whipped out his phone and scrolled through a few pictures. "Like this?"

"Yeah, that's it. That's the car exactly!" She

offered a lopsided smile. "I guess they aren't really circles. Only…" She squinted at the picture, straining to reconcile what was still off. "The license plate. The car didn't have a front license plate like this one."

"You did good." Jake turned the phone so Sam and the P.I. could see. "A Buick Enclave. The chief just bought this one."

"And we can narrow down the search to the states that don't require front license plates," Sam added.

Kara pictured the men at the river once more. "I remember something else. The man handed the adoption agency guy a bulging, half-page–size envelope, and there was a logo in the corner."

"Can you describe it?" the P.I. asked.

"Yeah, it was solid red with yellow words."

Jake's gaze snapped to Sam's. "A bank logo, maybe?"

"Yes." The P.I. tapped the tip of his pen to his pad with a grin. "This gives me lots more to go on."

Sam pressed two fingers to his ear and his attention instantly shifted to the hills behind Kara. "Copy that," he said brusquely into his mic then motioned them up. "Okay, we've got to move. Now!"

Kara's pulse kicked into overdrive at the urgency in his voice.

Jake grabbed her hand and sprang to his feet as the P.I. hurriedly gathered his photos. "I appreciate you meeting with me." A breeze caught the corner of one of the photos and sent it skittering off the end of the table.

Kara stretched to grab it.

"Leave it," Jake hissed, tugging her to move before she'd untangled her legs from the picnic table.

An odd *pop-pop* cracked the air.

"Down!"

"Down!"

"Down!"

The shouts came from every direction as she slammed into the ground, fought for breath... under the...bone-crushing...pain. Shots exploded around her.

A heavy weight pressed over her body. "You're okay."

Jake. If she could...just...catch...a...breath.

"You're going to be okay," Jake repeated more urgently, inching higher, shielding her head, not sounding convincing.

She tasted dirt and—*blood*. The light faded and understanding rushed in. She wasn't okay.

ELEVEN

The female deputy ducked behind the baby stroller and shot in the sniper's direction, providing cover. But nothing could shield Jake from the castigation lashing his chest as he hooked his arms under Kara's shoulders and dragged her behind the nearest tree. He never should've let her come here. He'd told her he'd protect her.

"Shots fired," Sam barked into his radio. "Two men down. Send ambulance and backup to…"

"Two?" Jake's gaze snapped to his brother upending the picnic table. The P.I. lay sprawled in the dirt behind him. "How is he?" Jake hissed, fumbling over the zipper on Kara's jacket.

"Bad." Sam dragged the man closer to the table's cover, leaving a smeared trail of blood in his wake as the shooting mercifully stopped.

"Find the wound and apply pressure until the ambulance gets here," Jake barked, then, giving up on Kara's zipper, ripped open her jacket to find the wound. "Kara, honey, talk to me." The sight of her ashen face caught him by the throat. "You can*not* die on me!"

She let out a shuddered moan.

"That's it." He stroked dirt-encrusted hair from her face, rechecked her airway, her breathing. "Talk to me."

Her eyelids fluttered, but failed to open. "Hurts," she moaned, her tongue flicking over a cut on her swollen lower lip.

"I know, baby, but stay with me. I need to turn you over." He'd already felt the hole the bullet had ripped through her jacket. A rifle shot, even at that distance, would've torn right through her if...

"Ow," she moaned as he rolled her gently onto her side, easing her arm out of the Kevlar vest.

His breath rushed from his lungs at the sight of the shattered ceramic trauma plate that Sam had stuffed into the level IV vest. But there was no blood. No blood!

He edged the bottom of her shirt up her back, revealing an angry red welt from the impact. He palpated the ribs, checking for broken bones.

Her moan clawed his heart raw. "I'm sorry, Kara." He eased her onto her back once again. "You've suffered an impact trauma, but the bullet didn't penetrate." His gaze caressed her too-pale face as he pulled her coat closed over her chest. "You're going to be okay."

"Easy for you to say," she groaned. "Let the

entire Seattle Mariners lineup have batting practice on your back, then we'll talk." The corner of her lip tilted up as her eyes finally slid open.

Humbled by the sight, for a moment he could do nothing more than drink it in. "You are a remarkable woman." He leaned over her and gently brushed his thumb along her bottom lip in a feathery caress, savoring the baby softness. Her breathy sigh flitted over his skin, sending his pulse charging.

Her long lashes swept her cheeks, and then the direction of those fathomless blue eyes dipped to his lips.

He forgot how to breathe. He leaned closer, then…

An explosion of sirens snapped him out of the fantastical world he'd tumbled into. He straightened regretfully, touching her cheek as he withdrew.

Sam was hunched over the P.I.'s chest, blood staining his hands. The female deputy stood guard, scoping the horizon. The other deputies had disappeared.

"Did they get the sniper?"

"He got away," Sam said through clenched teeth. "How's Kara? Does she need to go to the hospital?"

Kara rolled onto her side and pushed herself

to her knees, muffling a groan. "No, it won't be safe."

Sam shifted his gaze to Jake's, seeking confirmation.

An impact of that magnitude had to have compressed her ribs a fair amount, maybe caused some internal bruising in addition to the external. She'd be sore for a long time, but not enough to risk sending her to the local hospital if that sniper was still on the loose. "She'll be okay," he muttered.

"Okay." Sam turned to the female deputy. "Get them out of here. Make sure you're not followed."

"This way." She motioned to the run-down van parked at the edge of the parking lot, authentic looking for the cover of a young mother but not exactly a good getaway car, not to mention pretty easy to track.

"Go!" Sam shouted.

Jake scanned the hills one last time, then scooped Kara into his arms and hurried after the deputy.

Her arms laced around his neck, clinging tighter with every jolting footfall.

"We're almost there," he soothed.

The deputy flung open the side door, and Jake eased Kara onto the nearest seat, then jumped in.

"Okay, go!" He slid the door home. The van immediately lurched into Reverse. Bracing his knee against the seat, he fought to stay on his feet as he fastened Kara's seat belt.

Her eyes were pinched closed, her face contorted.

He pressed his lips to the lines creasing her forehead, wishing he could take away her pain as easily as he could kiss away his son's boo-boos.

An undeserved "thank you" whispered past her lips, twisting his heart.

"You might want to belt yourself in," the deputy said from the front seat, backing the van into a swift swerve that sent him toppling.

"Take it easy. You don't want to attract attention!"

She eased off the gas and cut through a subdivision. "Where am I going?"

Uneasy about giving a stranger—deputy or not—his address, he expelled a breath. "Drive around for a bit. Make sure no one is following us."

She zigzagged through subdivisions, giving the direction the sniper had been a wide berth.

"Jake," Kara puffed out with obvious effort, although her voice was scarcely audible. "He's seen me with you. I can't—" She gulped a mouthful of air. "I can't put you in any more danger."

Her unselfish concern flowed through him like the homespun warmth of hot cocoa on a crisp winter's day, and he couldn't help the altogether inappropriate smile that tugged at his lips. "If our sniper's already made that connection, it's too late to protect me. And I'll feel a whole lot better knowing where you are."

"But—" Her voice petered out and her tortured gaze clung to his. "But Tommy," she finally squeaked out.

As if a Mack truck had hit him square in the chest, Jake's breath rushed from his lungs. He closed his eyes and his son's smiling, trusting face danced before him. *Lord, I can't endanger my son.*

The image of Jesus on a cross seared his thoughts.

Oh, God... His mind blanked. *How do I pray? What do I do?*

Instantly he remembered his uncle's cabin in the foothills. He pulled out his phone and called his dad. "There's no time to explain. Pack up enough food and clothes to last at least a few days and get everyone to Uncle James's. Make sure no one follows you. We'll meet you there."

His dad quickly agreed and hung up.

"What are you planning?" Kara whispered.

"Do you trust me?"

Her throat worked up and down and, for an agonizingly long moment, he feared she might say no. Finally she nodded.

He squeezed her hand. "Hang on a little longer

and we'll get you to someplace more comfortable." He phoned his uncle James and quickly arranged to borrow his cabin in the foothills and his old pickup to get them there. "If Dad beats us to your place, can you help him load everything into the truck? Make sure it's gassed up."

"Sure thing. What's going on?" Uncle James asked.

"I'll have to fill you in later. I appreciate this." Jake clicked off before Uncle James could press for more answers.

The female deputy met his gaze in the rearview mirror. "Where to?"

His wariness at revealing even an interim location to this virtual stranger reared its ugly head once more. He scrubbed a hand over his jaw. The reality was she could access his DMV records, and thereby his home address, in all of thirty seconds, and probably those of every relative within a thirty-mile radius—just like the sniper if he had the right connections. Jake spit out the address and made a mental note to borrow his uncle's rifle, too.

Pain dragged Kara from her dreams. She rolled onto her side and frowned at the empty chair next to her bed. Had it been a dream? For a few blissful moments, Jake had been looking at her the same way he had after she was shot—with his heart in his eyes. Back at the park, his relief that she was alive had quickly transplanted the fear and guilt swirling in his smoky blue eyes, but not the heart-stirring vulnerability. No man had ever cared what happened to her so much that he'd look as if he'd shatter if she died.

She trailed her thumb over her lip, remembering the fire his touch had ignited in her and the scarcely banked heat in his gaze as he came so close to kissing her. She curled the blankets in her arms and balled them against the ache in her chest. It'd been the adrenaline, the life-or-death urgency of the moment. That was all. He couldn't care for her. Not when she'd done nothing but endanger his family. Tommy's disappointment after they'd arrived at the cabin when he'd learned he couldn't play outside had been bad enough, but the fright in his eyes when his grandfather and Jake had loaded their rifles had nearly undone her.

Okay, had totally undone her.

Mrs. Steele must've slipped a sedative in with the pain pills she'd given her, because somewhere in the middle of her begging Jake to just drive her to the marshal's office and be rid of her, she'd grown too dopey to fight.

"Now that I'm rested, I won't take no for an answer," she said to the empty room.

Something rustled at the side of her bed, and

an instant later Rusty plopped his curly-haired head on her sheets and gazed at her with honey-brown eyes that seemed to say, "But I don't want you to leave."

She ruffled his fur. "I'm going to miss you, too, boy." She gingerly eased off the bed to minimize the jar to her aching back, then edged aside the corner of the curtains in the room's lone window. Darkness blanketed the forest in a shadowy shroud. How long had she been asleep?

She squinted at the night table, the top of the bureau, the walls, but couldn't find a clock, at least not one that she could see in what little light the night table lamp emitted.

Ambling toward the bureau, she finger-combed her hair. Rusty stayed glued to her side. She chuckled. "Let me guess. Jake charged you with making sure I didn't escape." She stopped in front of the bureau and, hiking up the bottom of her top, twisted to see her back in the mirror. She winced at the movement as much as at the sight. Rusty whined. How had one tiny little bullet given her a bruise the size of a dinner plate?

The door creaked open. "Oh, good, you are up. I thought I heard—" Jake's cousin's gaze met Kara's in the mirror, then dropped to her exposed midriff. "I'm sorry. I'll—"

"No, that's okay. Come in, please. Sherri, right? The paramedic?" Kara shoved down her top before Sherri backed out of the room with that delicious-smelling tray of food.

"That's right." Sherri hitched up her elbow and tipped on the light switch as she kicked the door closed behind her. "I thought you might be hungry."

"Famished, but I can come out to the table to eat."

The cabin shook with the slam of a door.

"Um." Sherri's gaze flicked to Kara's closed door. "It's probably better that you stay in here for a bit."

Raised voices sounded from the other room.

"What's going on?"

Sherri set the tray on the bureau. "Sam's here."

Kara's pulse quickened. "With the marshal?"

"I'm not leaving her," Jake's angry voice boomed through the door.

Sherri's lips pressed into a flat line, apology in her eyes. "Sam sent Tommy and his folks home," she whispered.

"Without the dog?" Her heart deflated. "Oh." It wasn't safe for the dog to be seen, let alone associated with his family.

"Sam brought me here, because he thought you might appreciate some female company until—"

"You. Have. No. Choice." Sam loudly enunciated each word as if Jake were a simpleton. "What were you thinking bringing her here?"

"Keeping her safe," Jake growled. "What do you think I was thinking?"

Kara cringed at Jake's hostile tone, hating that she was the cause of him and his brother being at odds.

"*Your* plan obviously didn't work," Jake continued. "How did that shooter find her at the park? Huh?"

"We think he tracked the P.I. through his phone's GPS." Sam's voice grew quieter, and Kara had to strain to make out his words.

Ignoring Sherri's urging to sit down and eat, Kara opened the door a crack and peeked out.

Sam and Jake alone occupied the room, their foul moods a stark contrast to the homey atmosphere of the cedar-scented log walls and crackling fire flanked by a circle of cozy-looking chairs.

Jake grabbed the cell phone Sam held. "And what makes you think he won't do the same with your phone? Or with that marshal's who you send up here? And how'd a P.I. from Boston find her in the first place?"

"His brother is a software geek. He's had face-recognition software trolling news and social media sites for Nicole look-alikes for the past three months. Within an hour of the hit on Hadyn's online edition of their newspaper, the P.I. was booked on a red-eye from Boston."

"Right. That sounds about as believable as a TV cop show. Chances are he's been working with the bad guys all along and his story was a cover to cajole her into talking so they could figure out how much of a threat she really is."

"Why?" Sam snatched back his phone and shoved it into his pocket. "Forty-eight hours ago her assailant was willing to burn her to death. You think he suddenly got a conscience?"

An icy chill slithered through Kara's body and a whimper slipped past her lips.

Jake's attention snapped in her direction. He strode toward her and helped her to the sofa. "You shouldn't be up. You need to rest."

Ignoring the flare of pain at the movement, she inhaled deeply to add backbone to her response. "What I *need* is to know what's going on. Is that P.I. going to survive? Will—" She hiccupped on a swell of emotion at the thought that, after all this, those poor parents might still not get their son back. She swallowed hard. "Will someone follow up on the information I gave him?"

"Yes," Sam reassured. "The FBI already is. And—" he threw a glare at Jake "—just so you know, the guy's story was legit."

She nodded, relieved to hear that, at least. "Do you think it will make a difference? What I remembered about that man's car, I mean."

"Absolutely." Sam pulled up a chair across from

her. "Hundreds of tips came in following the initial story three months ago, and hundreds more since this week's arrests. The FBI is narrowing in on any that might point to the kidnapped child, particularly those from Pennsylvania and Delaware, the closest states to Boston that don't require front license plates. Between the make of the car and the topaz—November—birthstone on the driver's ring, they can quickly look at which potential matches have also brought home a child in the past three months."

Kara's breath seeped from her lungs. Sam made it sound so easy. But as Jake said, those kinds of searches didn't have nearly the success rates depicted on TV. "And the birth parents will get their child back?"

"Yes. The adoption wasn't legal and, considering where the adoptive parents picked up the child, there was no way they didn't know it."

"So what happens to me now?"

Sam's jaw ground back and forth, his gaze flicking to Jake's. "We—" His cell phone rang. Glancing at the screen, he said, "Excuse me, I need to take this."

Kara looked to Jake. "Is a marshal coming for me?"

He clasped her hand, twining his fingers between hers. "Yes, but not tonight."

"I'm glad." She smiled up at him. Like a kid to

candy, her gaze shifted to his lips and heat rose to her cheeks. She ducked her head. "It's going to be hard to say goodbye to you and your family. You've all been so kind, made me feel..." She gulped down the admissions that seemed to spill too easily from her lips when Jake was around.

His thumb traced tiny circles over the back of her hand. "Made you feel what?" he whispered.

"When will the marshal come?" she blurted, desperately needing to change the topic before she read more into his tummy-rippling touch than he intended. Never mind how more at home she'd felt in his parents' home than she'd ever felt in her own. They were obviously just very caring people. Jake couldn't possibly have feelings for her. He scarcely knew her.

And she scarcely knew him.

Jake glanced at his brother, still on the phone. "I'm not sure when the marshal will get here. But you know, one day soon, they're going to catch this guy and you'll be free to live wherever you want. Do you think you might...?"

Sherri plodded into the room carrying the tray of food Kara had yet to touch and set it on the coffee table in front of her. "I thought you might want the food before it gets cold. Would you like tea with it?"

Kara slipped her hand from Jake's. "Sure."

"Can you make coffee, too?" Jake asked, plow-ing his freed hand through his hair. His gaze shifted to the darkness beyond the snug little cabin. His Adam's apple bobbed and he moistened his lips, his brow furrowing as if some inner war waged within him.

Rusty whimpered behind the closed bedroom door and scratched.

Sherri freed him and he promptly trotted over to Kara and sprawled at her feet.

While Sherri rummaged through the rugged pine cupboards in the kitchen area, Kara ruffled Rusty's ears. Gathering her courage, she whispered, "I'd like to come back."

Something bright jumped in Jake's eyes. "You would?"

"I would. As a teacher, I get summers off. So I could come for a long visit if your parents wouldn't mind. Or I could rent—"

The light in his eyes dimmed, as if—dare she think?—he might've been hoping for something more permanent.

Kara gave her head a mental shake. It was just the adrenaline-charged emotions. He still had his deceased wife's photo pinned to his truck's dash. If he hadn't felt compelled to *protect* her, he likely never would've given her a second look. Helping her was more about making up for his inability to save his wife. He'd practically said as much, more than once.

Never mind that, thanks to her, his son couldn't even take his beloved dog home.

Sam pocketed his phone, and motioned to Sherri. "Could you make an extra cup for me, too?" He reclaimed his seat across from Kara. "That was the marshal's office. Since I've assured them that you're safe here for the time being, they'd like to wait until Monday to relocate you. There are some new developments with the adoption agency case that could soon give them a bargaining chip to secure a name on the shooter. If all goes the way they hope, you may be free to return to Boston very soon."

As if swept up on an eagle's wings, her spirit soared. "Really?"

Sam smiled. "It's possible."

Jake squeezed her hand. "That's great news!"

Sherri joined them, carrying a tray of steaming mugs. "What's great news?"

Kara's heart jolted. She'd gotten so used to Jake and Sam knowing who she really was that she'd forgotten everyone else was still in the dark…and if things didn't transpire as the marshal hoped, they needed to be kept in the dark.

"The police have a lead on the shooter," Jake quickly improvised.

"Oh, that is good news." Sherri reclined in a chair and sipped her coffee. "An unsolved murder would hurt the town's—"

Kara choked on her tea, sputtered half of it out. "Murder?"

"Uh." Sherri's penitent gaze shot from Jake to Sam.

Kara slammed her mug on the table, scarcely registering the hot liquid that swelled over the brim. It didn't sting half as much as the zip-your-mouth glare Sam leveled at Sherri or the shuttered look in Jake's eyes. "What aren't you telling me?"

TWELVE

Haunted by the memory of Kara's anguish when they'd told her the P.I. hadn't survived, Jake punched his pillow then flopped onto his back on the too-short sofa and stared at the overhead timbers in the early-morning light. Sighing heavily, he folded his arms over his chest, wishing they had offered more comfort as he'd held Kara in her grief. Everything in him wanted to take away her pain. He hated that she blamed herself when she'd risked her life to try to help recover that little boy.

Jake clenched his fist against his pounding heart. If anyone were to blame, it should be him. From the beginning, he'd known in his gut that meeting with the P.I. was a bad idea. He should've tried harder to stop her.

Sam sauntered out of the end bedroom—the one Jake had deliberately drawn the short straw to avoid claiming. He'd figured that parked on the lumpy couch, at least he'd hear if Kara needed him in the night, even if he did nod off. Not that he had. The thought of her alone, in the dark, at the mercy of the day's events replaying in her dreams, had kept him awake all night.

"Shouldn't you be getting ready for work?" Sam asked.

"I already told you that I'm not leaving her." He'd made that mistake with April, acquiesced to assurances that everything would be fine. He wouldn't make that mistake again. He'd already made enough of them.

"And I told you that you're not doing her any favors by hanging around." Sam filled the coffee-maker and flipped it on. "If the shooter suspects a connection between you and Kara, he could be watching for you. The sooner he sees you returning to your regular routine, the more convinced he'll be that Kara's already been relocated."

Jake shoved off the sofa. "If you thought that, what on earth were you doing letting Mom and Dad take Tommy home?"

Sam poked at the embers in the woodstove, stirring them into flames as readily as he'd provoked Jake. "Because he hasn't seen *them*. You, on the other hand, had your face plastered across the newspaper with hers. So, if by chance, he did focus on you through his rifle scope, your presence might stoke his curiosity enough to watch for you."

"And risk him following me back here? Forget it." Jake stalked to the cabin phone and dialed the station's number to call in sick.

The chief was surprisingly empathetic. "Yeah, I'm sorry, man. Davis told me you had befriended her."

Jake blinked. "Pardon me?"

"The woman you rescued from the fire a few days ago. It was all over the news."

Jake broke into a sweat, slumped into the nearest chair. "What—" he swallowed the lump that had lodged in his throat "—was all over the news?"

"The shooting. Her death," he said, sounding confused by the question.

Jake felt the blood drain from his face. "Uh, right, of course." He blew out a breath. "I'm sorry. Not thinking straight. I didn't sleep last night."

"I understand. Hits too close to home with—" The chief sputtered before bringing up April's death, but the pain shot through Jake's chest as sharp as ever. "Well, you know. Take all the time you need. Davis volunteered to follow up on the investigation into last night's arson."

Jake ramrodded to attention. "There was another arson?"

"Yeah, our guy's picking up his pace. But at least there weren't any victims this time. It was an old barn out on Perry Road with nothing but rusted-out farm implements and musty hay inside."

"Any familiar faces in the gawkers?" The image of the bulbous-nosed man he'd seen watching Kara's home burn rose to mind.

"We took photos this time, like you suggested. I can email them to you if you want to take a look."

"That'd be great. Thanks." Jake turned on Sam the instant the chief hung up. "You told the media she died? And you're feeding me some cockamamie story about why I should go back to work!"

"Keep your voice down," Sam hissed. "It was the marshal's idea. He doubted the sniper would believe the story, but figured he'd conclude that they must've whisked her out of town or the story wouldn't fly. They're hoping it'll buy them an extra day to track down their leads and set up a new identity for her.

Jake unclenched his grip on the phone. "So *here* is the safest place for her to be."

Sam shrugged. "For now."

"Good." Jake stalked to the coffeepot, a plan forming in his mind to make the most of the time they had. Tomorrow she'd be on her way to who knows where and he'd be with his son at the Seattle Children's Museum for his long-anticipated first school field trip. And eventually, if she didn't return, he'd manage to forget the electricity that had charged through his chest at her touch. The jolt that had revived a part of his heart that hadn't beat for five long years.

Between his brother's case-related phone interruptions, they passed the day playing games, with Kara and him teaming up against Sam and Sherri. Jake's gaze strayed from the paper on which Kara was frantically drawing clues to her Pictionary word to the laughter in her eyes, the curve of her lips, the lamplight glistening in her hair like streaks of honey.

Was she really a brunette? Or was the color part of her cover as the brown contact lenses had been?

Apparently catching the distracted direction of his gaze, she waved her arms in front of his face and hammered her pencil tip to the picture she'd drawn. Her eyes flared, her lips pressed together as if it took every ounce of her self-control not to speak a clue.

Jake shot a quick glance at the clue Sam had drawn for Sherri and guessed, *"Pirates of the Caribbean."*

Kara rolled her eyes and added a sweeping mountain in front of the boat she'd drawn. At least he thought it was a boat.

"That's a boat, right?" he whispered. She nodded at him, looking like a tight-lipped bobblehead doll, and tapped the mountain with her pencil tip.

"Noah's ark," Sherri guessed, slanting a peek at Kara's paper.

Jake moved to block his cousin's view as the sand in the timer trickled to almost nothing.

Kara broke into another flurry of drawing and Jake couldn't help but laugh at how she shared his competitive streak. As a new mountain decimated the front of her boat and a stick figure swan-dived into the water, he yelled, *"Titanic!"*

Kara sprang to her feet with a whoop, her arms shooting up exultantly, and high-fived him. "I can't believe how long it took you to guess that!" She fell back onto the couch laughing.

His heart thrilled at the sound, grateful for the chance to help her forget, if only for a few hours, the danger she was still in.

She pressed her hand to her chest. "That was my favorite movie. I love how he makes Rose promise him she'll survive. No matter what."

Jake's muscles liquefied as his gaze drew hers. Holding it bound, he gripped the back of his chair, his heart demanding the same assurances of her.

Her eyes darkened to midnight, the silence raucous.

The insistent ring of Sam's cell phone caused them both to jump. Jake held his breath as Sam answered. Kara's gaze clung to his as if she were afraid to hope the news could be good.

"His battery was probably dead." Sam scowled

at Jake, and he suspected Sam was talking about his cell phone. He'd pulled the battery for fear the sniper would get his number and somehow track them here through his phone's GPS. "Yeah, he's right here. Just a second." Sam handed the phone to Jake. "Davis."

"Listen, Jake, I'm sorry to bother you, but we've got another arson on our hands."

"What?" Jake's pulse skyrocketed. He stepped away from the table, lowered his voice. "Same M.O.?"

"Long way from figuring that out. Just got the call, and with this wind, we could have a hard time knocking her down. I thought you might want to work the crowd. You know, look for familiar faces. Might get your mind off…"

Kara's anxious blue eyes followed him around the room. Not what he wanted to get off his mind by a long shot. Except for the anxious part. But no matter how remote the possibility that these arsons were connected to the fire at her house, he shouldn't pass up the chance to ferret the guy out. These kinds of firebugs usually hung around to watch their handiwork.

"Did you look at the photos from last night's scene?"

"Not yet." He hadn't wanted to risk firing up his phone to download the email. He glanced at his watch. Eight. Kara would be asleep by the time he got back, and he'd need to head out early in the morning if he wasn't going to disappoint Tommy and miss the field trip. Her head tilted as she watched him. Something told him she wouldn't mind being awakened early to say goodbye. "Okay," he said to Davis. "Give me the address. I'll be there as soon as I can."

The instant he tossed the phone back to Sam, Kara was on her feet. "You're leaving?"

"There's been another arson. I need to go, but I'll be back before morning." He steered her out of Sam and Sherri's line of sight and cupped her face. "You'll be safe here."

"I know." Her breath whispered over her moistened lips.

He slowly dipped his head, his gaze tangling with hers. Her sweet scent filled his senses and his heart suddenly felt too large for his chest. He brushed a soft kiss over her lips and savored their velvety softness.

She leaned in on raised toes and returned the kiss with a fervor that took his breath away.

He slid his hands to her back, his fingertips delighting in the baby-soft hair at the nape of her neck as he drew her closer.

She rested her cheek against his chest, and her breathy sigh of contentment made his pulse throb.

"This isn't goodbye, okay?" he whispered, pressing a kiss to her temple, to her hair. He held her for a long moment, not wanting to go, yet filled with hope that tonight they might catch this arsonist, and maybe Kara wouldn't have to leave.

Kara's palm pressed firmly against his chest. "You need to go."

He held her hand against his heart. "I'll see you later. Before…" He cut off the thought, not wanting to think about the marshal who'd be here in the morning to make her disappear.

An uncertain smile fluttered over her lips. "Yes."

Letting her go, he grabbed his coat off the hook and stalked out to his uncle's old pickup truck. He climbed in and bent his head over the steering wheel. *Lord, please show the police where to catch this guy. Let Kara be able to stay. I don't know if these feelings she ignites in me will go anywhere, but I'd sure like the chance to find out.*

He fired up his truck and swerved out of the driveway before he could talk himself out of leaving. As he bumped along the gravel road that would eventually wind its way to the highway, he glanced at the clock and in his mind's eye glimpsed his wife's smiling face in the dashboard light. Guilt panged his chest. He touched the spot where, in his own truck, her picture sat and swallowed the lump in his throat. What was he doing? The day he buried April, holding their infant son in his arms, he'd buried any desire to ever love again. The last thing he wanted to do was let another woman down.

Unbidden memories of Kara's kiss played on his mind. The feel of her arms around him, the taste of her lips, the pliant way they'd moved beneath his. The way he'd responded.

He shook his head. Of course he'd responded. He may not want to fall in love again, but he was still a man. A man who hadn't kissed a woman in five years. Add to that the fact he'd scarcely slept in days and had almost lost her more times than he wanted to contemplate. Was it any wonder that kissing her had felt so natural? Perfect, even?

He shoved aside the thought and focused instead on reviewing what he knew about their arsonist. By the time he got to the fire scene, the abandoned warehouse was fully engulfed in flames and, with the wind whipping up fiery sparks and dropping them dozens of yards from the source, it was all his station's crew and Hadyn's volunteer crew could do to keep it from spreading. Their one saving grace was that the weather had been so wet that the sparks did little more than smolder.

Before getting out of his truck, Jake quickly reinserted his cell phone battery and scrolled through the photos the chief had emailed from last night's fire. His adrenaline surged at the sight of the bulbous-nosed guy he remembered seeing outside Kara's house. He emailed it to Sam, telling him to ask Kara if she knew the man in the picture, then zipped up his jacket and trolled the line of spectators.

A couple of minutes later a text came back from Sam. No, sorry. She doesn't recognize him.

He bit back a curse and shoved his phone in his pocket. Okay, but that didn't mean the guy wasn't connected. Jake scrutinized the face of every person he passed, but without the benefit of streetlights, it was difficult to see anyone's face clearly. He stalked back to his truck and pulled out his Maglite. Time to see who'd pop.

He shone his light at the crowd and snapped a couple of photos with his cell phone. He glimpsed movement at the edge of the group and swerved the light toward it.

A kid jerked out of the beam and took off.

"Grab him," Jake shouted.

One guy cut the kid off and a second rammed him to the ground from behind. The burly guy curled his fingers into the kid's jacket and whirled him from the face-plant to his back in one move and rammed a knee into his chest for good measure. He gasped. "You?"

Jake shined the light into the kid's face. "Who are you?"

"Ryan Stokes. I'm sorry. I didn't count on the wind. I didn't think it would get so out of control."

"My no-good daughter's no-good boyfriend," the man holding the kid down growled. He shifted his knee from his chest and, grabbing the kid's coat, hauled his shoulders a foot off the ground. "You telling us you set this fire, boy?"

The kid's eyes went wild. "I had to do something to stop you from hitting her. Didn't I?" He rammed the butt of his hand square into the man's nose.

His bulbous nose.

As one of the sheriff's deputies caught the kid's arms and secured them behind his back, Jake stared at the guy nursing his nose. "I've seen you at every fire."

"That's why I set them," the kid yelled. "Every payday, because it's the only thing that keeps him out of the bar."

"Why you little—" The guy lunged for the kid's throat, and a second deputy grabbed him.

"It's true. He's obsessed with watching fires." The kid struggled under his own captor's hold. "If it weren't for the fires, he'd get good and tanked, then go home and beat up his wife and daughter."

Jake shot the guy a loathing look, his gut roiling at the uncomfortably familiar story. His father-in-law had been a mean drunk.

"C'mon, kid," the deputy said, "we'll sort this out back at the station."

"I'm not sorry." The kid's gaze bore into Jake. "What's a building compared to my girlfriend's life?"

Jake lunged at him, his hand fisting around the flashlight he blasted in his face. "A woman almost died in that Hadyn fire!"

The kid shrank. "I didn't set that. I swear! I only set them on his paydays, because he's so obsessed with fire that he'll forget about drinking."

"Then how do you explain last night's and tonight's?" the deputy interjected.

"He got fired Saturday and went straight to the bar. My girlfriend and I saw his truck there when we were coming home. I begged her not to go home, but she said she couldn't leave her mom alone or he'd get even angrier." As the deputy steered the kid toward a cruiser, the kid glanced back at Jake. "Don't you see? I love her. My life would be nothing without her. I'd do anything to keep him away from her. Anything."

My life would be nothing without... Jake stared after the kid, the pieces fitting together in his mind like a puzzle that finally made sense. What if the reason the attacks against Kara hadn't stopped with the adoption ring's takedown was because the adoption ring had never come after her?

It had to be the guy who bought the baby, because he didn't want to be found and forced to return him.

The chief clapped Jake on the back. "Great job. The sheriff just told me you fingered our man."

"Yeah, I'm sorry. I need to go." He raced back to his truck and pulled out his cell phone. "Sam," he said the instant his brother picked up. "It's not the adoption ring that's after Kara. That's why the attacks didn't stop after the takedown."

"What are you talking about? Who else would it be?"

"The guy who adopted the baby. The guy who Kara saw in the park in Boston. Don't you see? He and his wife finally have the child they've always wanted, and he'll do anything to make sure no one tears him away from them. Not Kara. And not that dead guy they found floating in the river back in Boston."

"I think you might be on to something."

Jake fitted his phone on the dash mount and pulled onto the road to head back to the cabin.

"Yeah," Sam repeated contemplatively. "It would explain why he took out the P.I., too. We'd be looking at someone with military training, communications know-how and serious connections."

"Or the money to buy them."

"Hmm. I'll call the marshal and let him know."

"Good." Jake glanced at his rearview mirror and turned onto the highway leading to the foothills. "I'll be back soon." As he jabbed Disconnect, a headlights' beam swept across his side mirror. He eased off the gas, an uneasy feeling churning in his gut. He'd noticed the car leave the scene right behind him. Hadn't thought anything of it, since lots of the fire watchers had started to head back to their vehicles after the kid's arrest. But what if Sam was right and the sniper had been watching for him? He'd lead him straight to Kara.

Jake signaled to pull off at the next gas station.

The car drove past.

Jake chuckled. Okay, well, better paranoid than sorry. He waited another minute, then turned back onto the road.

Half a mile farther on, a car suddenly appeared behind him again.

He squinted at the rearview mirror, but with the headlights beaming at him, he couldn't tell if the car was the same one. He glanced at the dashboard clock. It'd be close to midnight before he got to the cabin as it was. His chest pinched at the thought of not getting another chance to see Kara, but...

He flicked on his blinkers and made a U-turn. He couldn't take the risk.

THIRTEEN

At the sound of tires crunching gravel, Kara jolted up from her bed and instantly groaned at the ache in her back. Rusty, now alert at her feet, whined in commiseration. She pulled on a robe and hurried to the window, her heart too light at the thought of seeing Jake again to slow down. "You're such a sweetie," she whispered to Rusty as he trotted after her. "I'm going to miss you."

Her heart fell. Outside, a dark-haired stranger with a telltale bulge under his jacket stood chatting to Sam. The marshal. And Jake still hadn't returned.

She pressed her fingers to her lips, remembering the minty taste of his kiss, the possessive strength of his arms drawing her closer. Her heart fluttered at the memory of his whispered words—*this isn't goodbye.*

Her breathing quickened. Something must have happened to him.

She hurriedly dressed and then rushed into the main room, where Sherri was setting a platter of bacon and eggs on the table. "Where's Jake? Why didn't he come back?"

Sherri's expression turned empathetic. "I'm afraid he's not coming back."

"Not coming back?" she repeated dumbly, her heart thundering, her mind refusing to process what Sherri meant. "Did something happen to him?"

"No, nothing like that. He just changed his mind, I guess. Sam didn't really say. Maybe Tommy had been asking for him."

Kara's racing heart slowed. He was okay. *He was okay.* So why did she feel as if she'd just lost her best friend?

"I'm sorry."

Yeah, so was she. She numbly accepted the coffee mug that Sherri pressed into her hand. It had to be the kiss that had spooked him. He'd meant it to be something sweet, but when his lips touched hers, they'd ignited such a yearning for more she hadn't wanted to stop. He'd probably got scared she'd read more into the kiss than he'd intended. And who wouldn't worry?

She was a hunted woman.

Never mind that he still had his wife's picture

pinned to his dash—a constant reminder of the irreplaceable love he'd lost.

She took a gulp of coffee, welcoming the bitter taste.

"You all right?" Sherri slid into the seat beside her and passed the platter of bacon and eggs.

"Just nervous about moving on." She declined the offered food. "I don't think I'm up to a big breakfast."

Sam clomped in, shaking fresh snow from his hair. "Your marshal's here, Kara, and you're going to need to get going quickly. It's started to snow. The roads could soon be slick."

Kara eyed the tall stranger who'd scrutinized her from the instant he stepped inside behind Sam. "Where are you taking me?"

The man's gaze flicked to Sherri and back to her. "The airport."

She nodded, supposing she wouldn't get any more details until they were alone.

"Kara—" Sam motioned to the man "—this is Deputy Marshal Lewis Monson." Sam held her gaze. "You can trust him."

She ducked her head and swallowed. It had taken more than a day to give Jake her trust, and he'd saved her life. Twice.

Sam grabbed the newly "aerated" coat his mom had given her and held it out for her to slide her arms into, a move that even with his help roused the ache in her back.

Rusty leaned against her leg and nuzzled her hand.

She dropped to a crouch and gave him a big hug. Her heart rammed into her ribs as she whispered in his ear, "Give Jake and Tommy a big sloppy kiss for me, okay?"

When she stood back up, Sherri gave her a gentle hug, gingerly avoiding her bruises. "Take care, Kara. Keep in touch when you can."

Sam's lips pressed into a sad frown at Sherri's comment. When Sherri stepped back, Sam, too, pulled her into a hug. "Jake's sorry he couldn't come back to see you off," he whispered. "He was afraid someone was tailing him last night and didn't want the guy to track him to you."

She blinked back a sudden press of tears. Could it be that the feelings Jake's kiss stirred hadn't been one-sided after all?

She eyed the marshal who'd be whisking her away. If only she and Jake could've had more time to get to know each other, maybe…

She drew in a ragged sigh. Listen to her. When had a relationship ever given her anything but heartache? At least this way she could fondly carry her memory of her knight in shining armor in her heart. One knight who'd never get a chance to let her down.

The marshal escorted her to his black sedan, his silence unnerving.

You can trust him. Sam's declaration echoed in her mind, but her stomach only churned harder as the click of the electronic door lock reverberated through the car and the deputy marshal donned dark shades despite the sunless day.

She shivered at the icy sleet that melted off her hair and slid under her collar.

Before they were a hundred yards from the cabin, he started a rundown of the rules for her new identity—Connie Klumchuck of Wisconsin, a cheese factory worker. "But I guess you know the routine," he finished.

"Yeah, not that it stopped them from finding me last time."

"Trust me. No one's going to find you by the time I'm done with you."

Kara's breath stalled in her throat.

He chuckled. "I guess that sounded a little ominous. I meant you have nothing to worry about. I've never had a witness compromised."

Kara forced the breath into her lungs. "Sam said the police had some leads on who's been after me. Do you think I might be able to go home soon?"

He shook his head. "I've never had a witness want to go back. The mob has a long memory."

"But I didn't witness anything to do with the mob. It was an adoption ring."

He shrugged. "Sounds like organized crime to me. I'm not up to speed on the case history. Your friend said they were working on a theory that one of the adoptive parents put a hit on you."

She caught the dash as he swerved onto the highway, fishtailing on the icy road as frantically as her heart careening in her chest. The guy she'd photographed. Of course. A wannabe father would do anything to be with his child. Thinking of her own father, she buried her fisted hands under her armpits and focused on the barren hills whisking by. A wannabe father would do anything. Her father apparently hadn't *wanted* to be one.

They drove in silence until the deputy marshal skidded to a stop at the intersection of the main highway out of Stalwart that would take them to Seattle. Traffic was moving like molasses thanks to the slush on the roads. A school bus passed followed by a convoy of cars, reminding Kara of the field trip Tommy and Jake were on. The cars hugging the bus's tailgate were no doubt the parents who'd volunteered to chaperone. Her pulse picked up as she scanned the convoy for Jake's truck. How many schools were in Stalwart?

Another school bus inched through the intersection, and two cars later the line ground to a halt. The marshal took the opportunity to swing onto the road ahead of the next car, and the line soon resumed its slow crawl.

The marshal whipped off his sunglasses and tossed them on the seat, glanced in the rearview mirror then at the dashboard clock, his sudden antsiness making her even more nervous. "At this rate, we'll miss your flight."

"Where's my new ID?"

"In the trunk. I'll get it out when we get to the airport." He leaned sideways, apparently trying to see past the school bus, and then growled, "If we ever get to the airport."

The line of vehicles ahead began to accelerate through the next intersection. Then suddenly brake lights snapped on and horns blared as an out-of-control car skidded through the red and slammed into the side of the school bus.

"Oh, no." Kara gasped.

"Figures." The deputy marshal turned on his left signal, looking as if he'd try to pull up to the crash. He swore. "The stupid lady's blocking the whole road." He swung his arm over the seat and backed to within inches of the car behind them.

"What are you doing?" she screamed.

"Getting you out of here."

Ahead of them, the bus's emergency door had already popped open and parents were rushing to the bus to help out the children. She was a teacher. She knew the routine. She shouldn't just be sitting here. She unsnapped her belt. "We need to help!"

"We need to get you out of here." He cranked his wheel a hard left and eased forward, but couldn't clear the bumper of the car ahead of them. As he threw his shifter back into Reverse, she found the door lock release. "Those kids are terrified. I'm not running away." She shoved open the door and jumped out as the car jerked backward.

"Nicole, wait. It could be a trap!"

One foot already out the door, Kara stared across the car's front seat at the marshal. "Are you kidding me? You think this creep just *happened* to have an old lady sitting at that intersection, waiting for the chance to plow into a vehicle three cars ahead of ours?" She didn't even try to tone down her voice's rising pitch. "As if he knows which car is ours." She jumped out and raced to the back of the bus, icy sleet pricking her cheeks.

"Kara!" A little boy's voice came from inside the bus. Tommy squeezed past the child at the rear door and jumped into her arms. "You came back!" He clung to her neck.

"Just for you, buddy." Ignoring the ache in her back, she cradled his head and inhaled his little-boy scent. "Let's get you to where it's safe."

"Daddy!" he shouted gleefully.

Kara whirled on her heel with Tommy still in her arms, and her gaze slammed into Jake's.

His face lit and her name came out as the barest whisper as he swallowed her and Tommy in his arms. "I was afraid I'd never see you again." His warm embrace chased away the chill that had gripped her at the sight of the accident. He pressed a kiss to her hair, and then slid his palm to her cheek as he pulled back and drank her in.

Mesmerized by his gaze, she scarcely noticed the people jostling them out of the way of the door until the deputy marshal grabbed her arm.

"Kara, put the kid down," he hissed. "We need to go."

Jake hauled back his fist and Kara quickly pushed Tommy into his arms before he flattened the good guy.

"It's okay, Jake. He's my escort." She pried Lewis's fingers from her arms. "This is Sam's brother."

Jake hoisted Tommy onto his hip without taking his eyes off the deputy marshal.

Lewis offered a terse nod toward Jake. "It's not safe here."

"You need to get him into your truck," Kara said to Jake. She reached to pull Tommy's hood up against the nasty sleet and pressed a kiss to his cheek. "Give Rusty a big hug for me every night. Okay?"

"When will I see you again?" he whined, and Jake's gaze shifted to her, his expression sympathetic.

She brushed melting sleet from Tommy's cheek and mustered a smile. "I don't know, buddy, but know that I want to. Okay?"

"I want to go with Tommy," another little boy yelled, reaching toward Jake from the arms that held him.

The adult holding him said, "Can he sit in your truck with Tommy until we get another bus out here to take them back?"

"Sure." Jake hoisted him into his other arm, apology in his eyes as he turned back to Kara.

"Okay, let's go," the marshal repeated.

Kara shrugged off his hold. "I'm not leaving until every child is safely off the bus. It would go faster if you helped, too, you know."

"I'll be right back." Jake jogged toward his truck with the boys, and by the time Kara had helped three more children off the bus and across the ditch a safe distance from the wreckage, he was back. "I locked the boys in the truck and told them to stay put."

The deputy marshal stepped across the ditch with another child and set him beside the three Kara had escorted to where a teacher was taking a head count. "Okay, that's the last one. Let's go," he said to Kara.

Jake squeezed her hand and brought it to his lips. "Take care of yourself."

She hugged him and, stretching onto her toes, whispered in his ear, "Connie Klumchuck of Wisconsin. Look me up sometime."

He turned his head, his grinning lips brushing hers. "I'll do that."

The marshal yanked her arm. "We're done here."

Jake motioned to the teacher with the clipboard. "Yeah, I need to let her know I've got Tommy and his friend in my truck."

As the deputy marshal escorted Kara back to his sedan, she craned her neck to scan the row of vehicles behind them, hoping to spot Jake's truck so she could wave to Tommy one last time.

At the sight of a black truck door yawning open, her heart lurched. "Jake!" she shouted, sprinting for the truck.

The marshal caught her by the coat, then the wrist, and, pulling her close, hissed in her ear, "We gotta go. Now!"

Jake raced by her, shouting Tommy's name as she struggled to break Lewis's hold. The panic in Jake's voice cut off her breath. Wild-eyed, he peered through car windows. Others joined him, calling Tommy's name.

"Let me go," Kara yelled at the deputy marshal. "I need to help." Several cars in the line behind them had already pulled out and turned back to Stalwart. Others were flipping on signals to follow suit.

The little boy who'd been with Tommy scurried from across the ditch and held out a phone, tears streaming down his cheeks. "The man said mommy was on the phone."

Jake dropped to one knee and gripped the boy's arms. "What man?"

The marshal's grip tightened on Kara's wrist, but she dug in her heels. There was no way she could leave Jake like this, not after all he'd done for her.

"The policeman," the boy sobbed. "He pushed his badge at the truck window. Handed me the phone, but I couldn't hear Mommy."

Full-blown panic exploded in Kara's chest. The police weren't here yet.

Jake took the phone from the boy. "Where's Tommy?"

"Don't know." The boy's chest heaved heart-rending gasps. "I got out of the truck to try to hear Mommy. And then…Tommy was gone."

"Get in the car. Now!" the marshal hissed in Kara's ear, and lifted her off her feet as he shoved her toward the door.

"I ca—" The protest lodged in her throat at the

fury in his face and the realization… *Oh, please, God, no.* Her muscles liquefied, her legs betraying her. If not for his strong grip, she would've crumpled.

Was all this her fault?

Behind them, the cell phone Jake took from the boy chimed the tune "Somebody's Watching Me."

A chill, colder than any sleet, slithered down her spine.

"Where's my son?" Jake roared into the phone. His gaze snapped to hers, his expression horrified.

Her heart plummeted. This *was* her fault.

"Let me speak to Nicole Redman," the gravelly voice on the other end of the line growled.

"Ni—" Jake's chest seized. Tearing his gaze from Kara, he said, "I don't know anyone by that name. Where's my—?"

"Really?" He chuckled. "I guess I'm not surprised. She's the woman you were just hugging. If you want to see your son again, put her on the phone."

The deputy marshal's car, carrying Kara—aka Nicole Redman—started to edge out of the line of cars. Jake sprinted toward it and slapped his hand against the passenger window. "You have to take this call!"

In the driver's seat, the marshal shook his head and cranked the wheel a hard left.

"Stop!" Jake grabbed the door handle but the car jerked forward, ripping the handle from his grip.

"Stop!" Kara screamed at the marshal, and lowered her window.

Jake shoved the phone at her. "He has Tommy."

The marshal failed to clear the bumper of the car ahead of him and suddenly reversed. "Get rid of the phone," he hissed, slamming the shifter back into Forward.

Sheriff's cars careened up the other lane, blocking him in. He jumped out of the vehicle and flashed his badge as Kara slipped out the passenger door, her face pasty-white. "He says we have to lose the marshal. Then he'll call again, tell us where to meet him for the—" her voice broke "—exchange."

The word slammed Jake's gut like a sucker punch. For a full three seconds, he couldn't suck in enough air to respond. "He expects me to hand you over to get my son back? Kara—" Pain gripped his chest like a vice. "I can't do that."

She pushed him toward his truck. "He isn't giving you a choice."

Sam cut in front of them, the marshal behind. "What's going on?" Sam asked, his palms raised in a placating gesture that made Jake want to ram him into the ditch.

His fingers curled into a fist. "He took my son and he won't give him back until he has Kara."

The marshal, now flanked by two sheriff's deputies, grabbed Kara's arm. "We're going."

"No!" She kicked and flailed, fighting his grip like a wild woman. "I can't. This is my fault!"

With hands on their sidearms and gazes scanning for danger, the sheriff's deputies surrounded her as if protecting the president himself.

Jake grabbed her by the shoulders and she stilled. "The marshal's right. Go. There's nothing you can do here." The order came out more harshly than he'd intended, thanks to the fear gnawing through his chest like an insatiable beast.

"I'm sorry, Jake. I'm so sorry."

Her shattered expression would've carved a hole in his heart if it weren't already ravaged. "I need to take care of my son now. At least I'll know you're safe."

Sam ordered his men to check cars and get descriptions from drivers of every vehicle they could remember leaving.

Kara continued to fight the marshal as he forcefully edged her away. "But what if he won't tell you where Tommy is?"

The desperation in her voice shredded what

was left of Jake's patience. They were wasting time. He stalked toward her and snatched back the phone she still held. "We'll trace his call." He glared at the marshal. "Get her out of here."

She crumpled, her fight gone.

Unable to face the hurt in her eyes, Jake spun on his heel and thrust the phone at Sam.

"I'm sorry, Jake," she mumbled at his back.

Thankfully, the marshal shoved her into his car and ordered the deputies to clear a path.

"You can get a trace, *right?*" he demanded of Sam.

Sam wasted no time thumbing through the call history to get the number of the last caller. "Didn't Mom say she'd lend Tommy her phone for the day, just in case you were late joining the field trip and needed to find him?"

"Yeah!" Jake whipped out his phone. Why didn't he think of that sooner? He pulled up the app that pinpointed the location of their mother's phone. "He's headed for the state park."

"Okay, get in your truck and follow me." Sam sprinted for his car, barking orders into the radio on his shoulder.

Jake clutched his steering wheel in a death grip. *Please, Lord, don't let this man hurt my son.*

FOURTEEN

Kara stared numbly at the crushed front end of the car that had hit the bus as the marshal edged his sedan around the accident scene.

"I'm sorry, Nicole, my job is to keep you alive. Here—" He turned on his police radio. "You can follow their search at least."

Kara prayed Tommy's kidnapper wasn't doing the same or he'd have little trouble staying one step ahead of them. Would he let Tommy go once he figured out the marshal wouldn't let her take his bait? She gasped. "He had to know that the odds of my doing what he asked were a long shot."

"Yeah, he's an idiot if he thought any marshal would consent to an exchange…." His voice petered out.

"Exactly. So why try? He must have already been tailing us to see me with Jake and Tommy."

"Or tailing Jake. But he wouldn't have been

able to get a clear shot and make a clean getaway with everyone racing around."

"So why take Tommy?" She straightened, peering through the windows of every car they passed. "Why not bide his time and keep following us once traffic got moving again? Why risk losing sight of me?"

"Could be a diversion. If he's got a partner—" the marshal eased off the gas and scanned the sides of the highway ahead "—one of them could have taken Tommy to keep the cops busy while the other set up an ambush."

The frenzied updates over the police band attested to the fact that every available law enforcement officer not working the accident was focused on the kidnapping.

Lewis scrutinized the rearview mirror, and then punched something into the GPS mounted on his dash. At the next road, he suddenly veered left.

"What are you doing?"

"Changing routes. Just in case."

It seemed to her the road he chose was heading toward the mountains, not Seattle, and the sleet melting from her hair down her back suddenly wasn't the only thing making her shiver. What if *he* was the bad guy's partner?

She tried to swallow past the panic strangling her throat. "What about my flight? Won't that make us too late?" Not that she cared about the flight, only what else he might have in mind.

"There's no way we'd have made it after that delay."

An excited shout blasted over the radio. "We found the kid's phone. Twenty yards from the parking lot at the east gate."

"They took him into the forest?" Kara clutched the armrest, staring at the icy sleet replastering the windshield as quickly as the wipers swept it away. "He'll die of exposure if—" She pressed a fist to her mouth at the thought of Tommy wandering the forest alone.

"There aren't any tracks. The sleet is coming down too fast," another deputy reported in.

Kara's mind flashed to the hide-and-seek game Tommy played with Rusty. Did Sam still have the dog with him? She grabbed the radio mic. "Sam, Sam!"

Lewis grabbed it from her hand. "What are you doing?"

"I know how they can find Tommy. You've got to let me talk to Jake."

"Not over the radio." He hooked it back onto its holder and tossed her his cell phone. "Call him. You'll find his brother's cell number in the call history."

Deciding she could probably trust Lewis after

all, she tapped Sam's name on the phone. Her pulse throbbed triple time with each unanswered ring.

"What is it, Lewis?" Sam's voice finally snapped in her ear.

"It's Kara, Sam. Do you have Rusty with you?"

"No, Sherri took him home. Why?"

"Ask her to bring him to the park as fast as she can. He can find Tommy. He's a good tracker. Tommy's been training him to find him."

"Kara—" Sam's frustration seeped into his voice "—I don't have time to—"

"Sam, he can do it. I know he can. Please."

His ragged sigh betrayed his doubts. "Yeah, okay. It's worth a try." He clicked off before she could say anything more.

"Take me to the park," she ordered the deputy marshal.

"Right," he scoffed. "Do I look like I want to spend the rest of my life as a shopping mall security guard?"

"Look, the reason I went to the police in the first place was to save a child's life. I'm not going to run away now when another boy's life is at stake!"

He shot her a glare. "You don't have a choice." The car skidded on the slick road and he returned his attention to driving.

Urgency welled in her chest. "I'm good with dogs. You must have read that in your files. I can find that boy. The dog listens to me." Silence. She gentled her voice. "Do you have a son, Deputy Marshal?"

The muscle in his jaw flicked and the car slowed.

She pressed her advantage. "Time is of the essence. In this sleet, the scent trail won't last long. And neither will that boy."

Lewis cursed and veered left on the next road, which, if her sense of direction was right, would take them toward the state park. "If I lose my job over this, I'll shoot you myself," he growled.

"I'll find him. You'll see," Kara vowed. She'd find him or die trying. No way would she let Jake pay for his kindness to her with his son's life.

What seemed like an eternity later, a parking lot full of cruisers came into view and her heart lifted. She clasped the door handle before the marshal hit the brakes. He grabbed her arm.

"Ah," she cried out. "That's my burned arm."

He clamped her wrist instead. "You don't leave this car without a vest." He slapped the door lock and, releasing her wrist, reached into the back-seat. "Here." He dropped a vest into her lap.

She quickly shed her coat and struggled not to wince as she fit on the vest. She started to put the coat back on, but he stopped her.

"Wait a minute. You'll look like a giant bull's-eye in that red thing." He rummaged through a duffel bag in his backseat and shoved a water-proof jacket at her.

She held up the oversize jacket. "And I won't look like a bull's-eye with *marshal* printed on the back of this one?"

"Keep up the hood and no one will know you're not a marshal."

At the sight of Jake dejectedly returning to the parking lot with Rusty, Kara jumped out of the car while still yanking on the jacket. "Didn't he pick up any scent?"

Jake jumped at her voice, but the shock of seeing her again didn't eradicate the hollow look in his eyes. "You shouldn't be here."

She grabbed the leash. "I can find him, Jake. Trust me."

"No!" He grabbed her wrist, a little of the fire returning to his eyes, as the marshal edged a protective circle around them, scanning the surrounding hills and forest. "It's a setup. He drove by and tossed the phone, knowing we'd track it."

"If he tossed it, he's been here." Her gaze drifted past Jake's shoulder, past Sam and a dozen deputies poring over a map spread out on the hood of a cruiser to the only unfamiliar car in the parking lot. "Whose car is that?"

"Stolen. Probably abandoned here."

"Yeah, maybe by the kidnapper!" Kara tugged the dog's lead. "C'mon, Rusty." She sprinted across the parking lot, Jake and the marshal on her heels.

"I tried the dog there, too," Jake said. "There weren't any tracks."

"The sleet would've covered the tracks by now." Kara twined Rusty's lead around her hand and pulled open the passenger door.

Rusty barked immediately.

"You smell Tommy, boy?" she asked excitedly. "Seek!"

The dog's nose dived to the ground, moving in ever-widening circles.

Jake's eyes widened. "Seek? That's the command?"

The dog bounded up a grassy hill to a clearing.

At the sight of a small, red knit mitt, Kara's hopes soared. She pointed. "Is that Tommy's?"

Jake's face lit. "Yes!"

She jogged Rusty to it, and his tail wagged excitedly. "Good boy. Seek Tommy. Seek."

Rusty let out a bark that sounded an awful lot like a whoop and raced through the clearing with Kara at a full-out sprint, Jake and Lewis trailing. He stopped at a tiny footprint and her heart felt lighter than air.

"He's here," Jake breathed, clutching Tommy's glove to his chest. "Tommy!"

Rusty set off again, yanking Kara's arm with a jolt. She stumbled and lost hold of the leash.

"I've got him." Jake sprinted past, his longer strides easily overtaking the dog's, as he shouted his son's name.

Lewis pulled Kara to her feet and they raced after them.

Sheriff's deputies started up the hill from the parking lot. She hoped they'd called in an ambulance to take care of Tommy. His clothes would've soaked through long ago, and in this kind of weather it wouldn't take long for hypothermia to set in.

Rusty stopped and nosed the ground in frantic circles.

"What's wrong?" Jake blurted.

Kara's heart clutched at the panic in his voice. "The kidnapper must've picked Tommy up to carry him. Here, let me take over again." Kara took the leash from Jake and led Rusty back to where he'd last had the scent. "Seek Tommy. You can do it."

Rusty veered left, and this time Kara was right with him.

A single shot split the air. Pain exploded in her shoulder. The leash slipped from her fingers as she sank to her knees.

"Kara!" Jake's shout sounded far off as another shot rang out.

She jolted at a vicious kick to the ribs. A black

haze settled over her vision, and she was vaguely aware of being dragged into the trees.

Jake's warm fingers closed around her too-cold hand. "Kara, talk to me."

"I'm fine," she choked out, and gritted her teeth against the pain, praying for one more breath. "Jake, go. Find Tommy."

"But—"

"Go." Tears filled her eyes. "Please."

Torn by the sight of Kara's blood staining the sleet-covered ground and the dog tugging at his arm, Jake couldn't make his legs move.

Deputies charged up the hill after the sniper. Sam and a pair of paramedics rushed toward Kara, her complexion impossibly pale.

The marshal gripped Jake's shoulder and gave him a hard shake. "You heard her. Go. Find your son."

Rusty barked his agreement and Jake lurched after him, yelling Tommy's name. *Please, Lord—* The prayer lodged in his throat. He had to play the hero. And what good had it done? He'd put his son in this danger.

Rusty suddenly stopped, his nose sniffing the air instead of the ground.

Jake's chest constricted. *Oh, God, don't let him lose the scent.* "Tommy! Tommy, where are you?"

The dog cocked his head as if he heard a response, and plunged into the trees.

A fire ignited in Jake's chest. "Tommy?" he shouted with everything in him, welcoming the slap of branches against his face.

Rusty slowed, began circling, his nose rooting through the decaying leaves.

"What is it, boy?"

Rusty whined, retracing the ground he'd just covered.

Sam crashed through the trees behind them and came up short. "Jake?"

Fresh fear clawed Jake's heart at the unbearable empathy in Sam's voice. "Did you catch the sniper?"

"Not yet."

Jake's fingers fisted around the dog's lead as he resisted contemplating what Sam *wasn't* saying and what that could mean for Tommy. "Tommy's here. I can feel it," Jake insisted. He scanned the woods, his ears pricked for the slightest sound.

The wind whispered through the leafless trees, their gnarled limbs mocking him. The dog plopped his butt at Jake's feet and cocked his head as if he, too, heard their taunts.

"Tommy!" Sam shouted. "It's your dad and Uncle Sam. If you can hear us, make a noise."

Jake held his breath. A lone crow cawed and then exploded from the treetops. "Tommy!" Jake yelled.

A haunted echo reverberated off the distant cliffs.

The dog's head cocked. Then suddenly he surged forward, tail wagging. Entire rear end wagging!

"He hears him," Jake said. "Tommy!"

Rusty raced over dead tree trunks, around boulders and up slick terrain as if there was no tomorrow. Jake had to let go of the leash to keep from slowing him down. Suddenly his barking grew muffled, then abruptly stopped altogether.

A new chill iced Jake's veins. He dug his boot toes into the slick mud and charged to the top of the hill. At the sight of a cave, he shot a glance at Sam.

Sam pulled his gun and motioned Jake aside. "Let me go first."

Jake's heart thundered as he fought the need to rush to his son. Letting himself get ambushed wouldn't save him.

"Jake!" Sam shouted an eternity later.

Jake rushed into the cave. The darkness blinded him.

Sam's voice echoed off the walls. "I need a paramedic here, now!"

Jake's heart clutched at the urgency in Sam's

tone. Stumbling toward the glow of Sam's phone, Jake zeroed in on the sound of Rusty's whimpers. He lay beside his boy, nosing his motionless body.

Jake skidded to his knees, and for an instant, he couldn't breathe. Then his first-responder training kicked in as he scarcely resisted the urge to scoop Tommy into his arms. "It's okay, Tommy. Daddy's here. You're going to be okay."

Rusty whimpered, pushing closer to Tommy as if he instinctively knew the boy needed his heat. "Good boy, Rusty. Good boy." Tears blurred Jake's eyes as he checked Tommy's airway, his breathing—too shallow, too slow—and his circulation. "He's like ice." Jake peeled off his own coat and tucked it around his boy, then scooped him into his arms. "We can't wait for the paramedics."

Sam grabbed Rusty's leash and used his phone to light the way out. "Okay, let's go."

Outside the cave, Jake paused to drink in the sight of his son. His lips, earlobes, nail beds were all blue, his hands mottled and his cheeks already as white as porcelain, but—Jake clutched him to his chest—he was alive.

"C'mon," Sam prodded.

Jake hurried after Sam as quickly as he dared, not wanting to trip with his precious bundle. *Thank You, Lord. Thank You for keeping him alive. Thank You for this goofy dog, as maddening as he sometimes is. Thank You for Kara's insist—* His heart squeezed at the memory of how he'd left her. *Oh, God, please let her be okay.* He struggled to breathe past the emotion swelling his throat. "Sam," he gasped, stumbling after his brother, clutching Tommy tighter. "Kara, is she okay?"

Sam didn't glance back. His knuckles were white on the hand clamping the dog's lead. The other hand held his cell phone in a stranglehold. "I don't know."

Jake didn't believe him. He pressed his cheek to his son's baby-soft hair and drew in a ragged breath. *Oh, God, not again. Please, not again.*

Voices sounded through the trees.

"Over here," Sam called, and a pair of paramedics appeared, carrying a scoop stretcher.

The paramedics set down the stretcher, opened thermal blankets. "It's about ten minutes to the ambulance. You want to just carry him out?"

Jake shook his head, clutching his son's chilled body tighter. "His breathing is too slow."

"You an EMT?" the paramedic asked.

"Firefighter. Jake Steele. This is my son, Tommy."

"Okay." The paramedic spread a blanket over the stretcher. "Set him down here."

Jake kneeled beside the stretcher and gently laid Tommy down. The paramedics immediately covered him with the other thermal blanket. "It's too cold to strip off his wet clothes here," the second paramedic said as he pulled a needle and tubing from his pocket. "I'll try to put the IV in his head."

Closing his eyes against the sight, Jake squeezed Tommy's hand. "Hang on, son. You're going to be okay."

The paramedic pulled a saline bag from beneath his armpit and hooked it to the tube. "We're good."

"Good." The first paramedic quickly intubated him, attached the bag and began squeezing. "Okay, sir—" Jake's gaze snapped up, but the paramedic was looking to Sam "—I need you to take this end of the stretcher so I can keep bagging him. *Dad* can stay by his side and hold the dog's leash."

Sam handed Jake back his coat and the dog's leash.

"Okay, all together—" the paramedic said, and they hoisted the stretcher.

Jake walked next to his son's prone body in a daze. The sound of air being forced into his little boy's lungs burned Jake's chest. His eyes stung.

They cleared the trees, and the wind and sleet bit at their faces. Sam's foot slipped on the slick grass.

"Keep a tight grip, men," the paramedic bagging Tommy shouted.

They soon neared the place where Kara had been shot, and Rusty dropped to his belly. Jake tugged on the lead, but Rusty crawled toward the bloodstained ground, whimpering.

Jake blinked back tears, stuffing down emotions he didn't have time for right now. His son needed him. He wound the lead around his hand and tugged the dog away. "How's the shooting victim?" Jake managed to choke out, unable to voice her name.

"On her way to Hadyn Memorial."

"But how is she?"

"Critical."

The bottom fell out of Jake's stomach. It wasn't as if he hadn't known it. He just hadn't wanted to believe it. "How long will it take us to get there?"

"We'll be taking Tommy to Seattle Children's Hospital."

"Oh." Resuming his place next to his son, Jake reached down and ruffled Rusty's head. "She'll make it," he whispered, then added, "You'll see," as much to convince himself as the dog.

After the longest ten minutes of his life, they finally reached the ambulance. Sam took the dog to his car and the paramedics shifted into high gear, cutting away all of Tommy's clothes, piling on flannel blankets, attaching oxygen to the bagging mask, connecting the cardiac monitor.

"Heart rate's dropping," the paramedic reported.

Jake's pulse skyrocketed.

"Jake, *Dad!*" The paramedic doing the bagging looked pointedly at Jake. "You said you're a firefighter, right? Can you take over the bag?"

Jake looked dumbly from him to his son's lifeless-looking body.

"Heart rate's dropped below sixty," the other paramedic said urgently. "We need to start compressions."

Jake blinked. "No!"

FIFTEEN

Kara beamed at Tommy in her arms, happy and unharmed. The next moment Jake swallowed them both in a bear hug. His breath whispered past her ears, "I was afraid I'd never see you again." She snuggled into his warmth, sliding her arms around him.

"Ow." Her eyes jerked open and she stared at the tube running out of her arm.

"Hey, take it easy" came an amused, familiar male voice. The bed dipped as he reached across her and untangled the tube. "The nurse is getting tired of fixing that."

"Jake?" she whispered, straining to turn his way, but managing only to turn her head. She gasped at the stranger smiling down at her.

"Afraid you'll have to settle for Wal-Mart's newest security guard. Or at least I would've been if you hadn't been such a fighter."

She blinked and memories crashed over her. The marshal. The accident. Tommy's kidnapping! "Did—" Her tongue stuck to the roof of her mouth.

The marshal cranked the head of her bed up a few inches, then held out a cup and steered the straw into her mouth. "Here, take a sip."

She squinted at the sunlight slanting through the window next to her bed and realized it must already be Tuesday. After wrestling down a couple of swallows, she pushed the water cup away. "Did Jake find Tommy?"

"Yes, he's in ICU. It was touch and go. Severe hypothermia."

She clutched her blankets and pressed her fists to her thundering heart. "But he's going to be okay?" He hesitated and her heart skipped over a beat. "Lewis?"

"The doctor is optimistic Tommy will pull through with no lasting damage. You did good, Kara. That dog is something else." Lewis set the cup back on the table. "And you were right. The paramedics said if they'd been much later getting to him, he wouldn't have survived."

A sob bubbled up her chest. "If I hadn't stuck around where I didn't belong, he never would've been kidnapped in the first place."

"Hey—" Lewis patted her hand "—don't blame yourself for what the bad guys do. You'll be happy to know we caught him, by the way. He won't give you any more trouble."

Hope lifted her spirits. "You mean I'm free?"

"Not quite." Lewis shut the door then scooted his chair closer to the bed.

His earlier warning—the mob has a long memory—preyed on her mind, and a soul-splintering moan seeped out from deep inside her. She'd exposed Jake and Tommy. What if the mob didn't forget them either?

Compassion filled Lewis's eyes. "We're close. We've confirmed that Tommy's kidnapper and the guy who shot you are one and the same— Rodney Johns."

"There was only one guy? I thought after Tommy was kidnapped there must've been at least two."

"No, Johns said he knew you wouldn't walk away, not after the way you defied me to help the kids off the bus."

She shivered at how coldly he'd used her compassion against her.

"Ballistics also matched his gun to the shot that killed the P.I. And the sheriff verified Johns is the man who shanked his men outside the coffee shop."

"And the fire?" Kara hugged herself, remembering how Jake had been there for her every time Johns struck.

"We're sure he was behind that, too. Although it may be harder to prove."

"Is that what you have to do to stop the mob from coming after me again?"

"Actually, Johns has no known mob connections. He's a communications expert with military training, and whoever hired him probably had inside connections. We're not sure if he was behind the bomb and murder in Boston or if the mob is connected in any way. Someone may have just wanted us to think so."

Kara's breath bottled up in her chest. "So you're saying you don't know *who* wants me dead?"

"I'm saying Johns isn't naming names. But our best theory is still that it's the guy you saw buy the baby. With the client records destroyed and his contact at the agency already dead, you're his only remaining threat."

"But you don't know who he is or how to find him." It wasn't a question, and she didn't bother trying to keep the hopelessness from her voice. The strains of Christmas carols seeped through the door, and the thought of how lonely the holidays would be as Connie Klumchuck weighed on her mind.

"Not yet, but we have solid leads." He glanced at his cell phone and thumbed in a response. "Don't you worry. Chances are good that by the time they spring you from this place, I'll be able to drive you to the airport and put you on a plane back to Boston. How does that sound?"

Her stomach flip-flopped. It actually didn't sound as appealing as it would've a week ago. "How long does the doctor think I'll need to stay?"

"Another couple of days."

Only two days. Would Jake come see her? Would he want to see her?

"You're lucky the bullet didn't hit any bone or nerves or you'd be stuck here a lot longer. Of course, the way you were bleeding out, let me tell you, I didn't think you had a chance. The doc said the bullet lodged under your collarbone and clipped the lateral something or another artery, but the repair went without a hitch."

"Can I visit Tommy's room?" She tried to sit up, but scarcely pushed herself an inch off the mattress before falling back, spent.

The marshal frowned. "Afraid not. He's at Seattle Children's Hospital."

Her heart sank even deeper. She desperately needed to see for herself that Tommy was okay. To tell Jake again how sorry she was for… everything.

The door edged open, and the way Lewis sprang from his chair drilled home why Jake wouldn't want her anywhere near Tommy. Someone still wanted her dead.

Someone who couldn't care less about the collateral damage.

Sam strode toward her bed and held out a bouquet of pink carnations. "These are from Jake."

She gasped, her heart soaring. "Thank you." She buried her nose in the blooms, even though she knew florist's carnations didn't share the honey-cinnamon scent of the ones she used to admire in the church garden. Did Jake know that pink carnations meant gratitude?

Could he really feel that when she'd been the reason his son was in danger in the first place?

She searched for a card among the buds. "No card?"

"Sorry." Sam pulled a chair up to the bed opposite Lewis. "He asked me to pick up a bouquet when I mentioned I was stopping by."

Kara stuffed down her silly disappointment as Jake's harsh words following the kidnapper's call replayed in her head. *Get her out of here. I need to take care of my son now.* She squeezed shut her eyes. "They're lovely. Please, tell him thank-you for me."

"How about I let you tell him yourself? He'd like you to give him a call in Tommy's room when you feel up to it. The marshal has the number."

Kara nodded, not daring to open her eyes for fear the tears pooling there would spill. And another memory rushed over her, warming her like a kiss of sunshine—Jake clutching her hand as she lay wounded on the ground when he should've been searching for his son.

"Hey—" Sam chucked her chin "—I have good news."

Her eyes burst open. "You do?" she said at the same time as Lewis.

"Yes, thanks to your description, we've identified the guy who bought the baby—a wealthy businessman from Delaware, born in November, like we'd guessed from the topaz stone you remembered seeing on his ring." Sam's face beamed. "Turns out that six months ago his wife had a stillborn baby and suffered severe depression after the loss. She was kept in a psychiatric ward for three months. The neighbors said that they'd heard rumors the baby had died, but the husband kept saying, 'There was just a little complication with the birth and she'd be right as rain soon.' So no one was sure what to think. But a couple of neighbors called in tips after the adoption ring story broke. Turns out the woman came home with a three-month-old baby the day after you saw the exchange in the park."

"Oh, the poor woman. She'll be devastated to lose another child."

"Sure," the marshal said, disgust tingeing his voice, "but she'd have to be beyond naive to believe that quick an adoption had been legal." He returned his attention to Sam. "Have the feds arrested them yet?"

"Uh." Sam pulled out his cell phone and glanced at the screen, and she had the niggling feeling he'd done so to avoid answering Lewis's question. Rising, he handed her the phone. "I think this one's for you."

"Me?" She hadn't even heard it ring.

Sam winked and motioned to Lewis. "C'mon, let's get a coffee and give the woman some privacy."

Trembling, Kara waited until the door closed behind them before answering. The sound of Jake's gentle voice turned her inside out. "Jake, I'm so sorry for what happened to Tommy. I—"

"Shh, Tommy's going to be okay." Except the crack in Jake's voice said Tommy wasn't okay yet.

A regretful sigh seeped from her chest. "It's my fault he's hurt."

"How are *you* feeling?"

Her heart squeezed at his concern and how graciously he avoided casting blame.

"Kara?"

"Sore. But Lewis says I might be released in a couple of days."

A long silence filled the gulf between them as hope that he'd ask her to stay succumbed to the reality.

"What will you do then?" he asked finally,

sounding beyond exhausted. She closed her eyes and tried to picture the joy in his eyes when they'd hugged outside the bus, but all she could see was the hollow look she'd seen in his eyes after Tommy was taken and hear his scathing *You shouldn't be here.*

She cupped her hand over her mouth to muffle a whimper. Then, letting her hand slip to her throat, she drew a fortifying breath. "I guess I go back to Boston."

The heaviness in Jake's heart deepened as Tommy remained limp in Sherri's embrace, scarcely looking at the stuffed monkey she'd tried to cajole him with. She tucked him back under the covers and set the monkey beside his listless son, then walked around the bed with open arms.

Jake stood and gratefully received her hug, wistfully wishing it was Kara in his arms.

"I'm sorry," Sherri whispered. "Have the doctors given you any idea how long it will take him to…be himself again?"

Jake scrubbed his hand over his face and sank into the chair beside Tommy's bed where he'd been keeping vigil for the past three days. "No, they said trauma can make a child detached from what's going on around him. And that each one reengages a little differently."

Sherri squeezed his hand. "He'll come around."

"I know he will." Jake blinked back tears that had been coming too easily these past few days. "I'm just grateful he's alive. I—" He pressed his lips together to contain the emotion storming around his chest.

Sherri rubbed his back. "And Kara's alive, too. And will soon have her life back, thanks to you. You did good, Jake."

Jake shook his head. "It wasn't me. It was all God. I didn't know where to look for Tommy. I never even wanted my parents to get that nutty dog." He swiped at his nose. "And I sure didn't know how to get him to find Tommy. I thank God that He didn't let Kara listen to me. That she came back—" He squeezed his eyes shut and held his breath until his emotions were under control. "She came back to help, knowing it was a trap. But God spared them both."

"Wow." Sherri bent down and retrieved the Bible that had slipped from his lap when he stood. "I expected you to be questioning why God let it come to that. Why didn't He just let the police nab the bad guys three months ago so she never would've had to leave Boston? None of this would ever have happened."

Jake's heart lurched. "But then I never would've met her."

Sherri grinned. "Have you told her how you feel about her?"

A breath that felt as if it had been pent up for three long days leeched from his chest. Standing, he leaned over his son and stroked a wisp of feathery blond hair from his forehead. "It wouldn't be fair to her."

"Excuse me?" Sherri sounded utterly confused.

Jake smoothed Tommy's sheets and continued without facing his cousin. "After April died, I didn't think I'd ever feel this way again. To be honest, I didn't really want to. I never wanted to let another woman down."

"You didn't let April down," Sherri insisted. "You can't spend your life tormenting yourself with what-ifs. God was in control then, just like He was out in the woods." Silence hung between them for a moment. "Sometimes He chooses to spare our loved ones. Sometimes He doesn't, for reasons only the Lord knows and I don't pretend to understand. We ask for things and rant at Him when He doesn't give them to us, but you know what Sam said to me after his crazy mission to arrest his now-fiancée?"

"What?"

"That the greatest blessings sometimes come through the darkest moments. Like you just said, if the police had nabbed those guys back in Boston, you never would have met Kara. And she is really great. You need to tell her how you feel."

Jake let out a ragged sigh, his fingers fisting

the sheets he'd just smoothed. "She has family in Boston, a life. I can't ask her to leave that for me, and as strong as my feelings are for her, even after such a short time, I couldn't uproot Tommy, take him from his grandparents and move across the country to be with her. It wouldn't be fair."

Sherri chuckled.

Jake spun on his heel and glared at her. "I don't see what's so amusing."

"*You.* I think you've finally come to terms with the fact that you didn't let April down, but your hero complex is as strong as ever. You're sacrificing your happiness to do what you *think* is best for Kara and for Tommy."

He gritted his teeth. "That's because I love them. And when you love someone, you put what's best for them ahead of what you want for yourself."

She rolled her eyes. "What's best for them? How do you know what's best for them? From what I hear, you ordered the marshal to take Kara away. That sure wasn't best for Tommy. And who in their right mind would have wished that house fire on Kara? But after seeing the two of you together, I'm convinced God knew exactly what He was doing. Maybe before you start getting all noble and sacrificial on the people you love, you should ask them what they want."

Tommy curled onto his side and faced them,

his eyes slipping open. "Where's Kara?" he whispered flatly, his voice as lifeless as his eyes.

Jake stroked his son's hair. "She's still in the hospital, but I'm sure she'll come see you as soon as she can."

Seemingly satisfied, his son closed his eyes again.

"Are you sure about that, Jake?" Sherri hissed. "Did you ask her to come? Last time I talked to her, she was feeling really guilty about what happened to Tommy. I wouldn't be surprised if she thinks you'd prefer not to see her."

"That's ridiculous. She saved Tommy's life! If anything, I don't want her to see him still so listless and go back to Boston blaming herself, like I've done over April's death for the past five years."

Sherri gripped the sides of her head, tangling her fingers in her hair. "Argh! Men!"

Jake blinked, too stunned to have a clue what he'd done wrong now.

She bolted to her feet and stalked to the door. "Just call her. Okay?"

She didn't wait for a response. Good thing, too, because he wasn't sure he agreed. In fact, he was close to positive he didn't. He'd picked up the phone a hundred times since talking to her Tuesday morning, wanting to beg her to stay in Stalwart, wanting to tell her how he felt. But it wouldn't be fair to put that kind of pressure on her, to make her feel as torn as he felt. Her family was in Boston. She must miss them and her life there terribly. All she'd known since moving here was loneliness, unhappiness and life-threatening, nightmarish days.

He cared about her too much to make her choose between him and her life in Boston.

His mind flashed back to what she'd said at the cabin. *It's going to be hard to say goodbye to you and your family. You've all been so kind, made me feel...* She'd choked up then, and had deflected his question about how he and his family made her feel.

His heart thundered in his chest. Suddenly everything in him wanted to—

Jake whirred toward a sound at the door. "Mom, Dad, just the people I need to see. Can you stay with Tommy so I can visit Kara? It's important."

The wary glance Mom slanted Dad sent alarm bells clanging in Jake's head.

"What's going on?"

Dad pulled him away from Tommy's bed and lowered his voice. "They might be moving her."

"Is she worse?"

"No, nothing like that. The FBI think they identified the guy who contracted the sniper."

"That's great news!"

"No. He hopped a plane to Seattle. Landed an hour ago."

Blindsided by the gravity in his father's voice, Jake back stepped. "They think he's coming after her himself?"

Dad squeezed Jake's shoulder. "The feds, the airport police, Seattle P.D., Sam's department, the marshal's office, everyone is working to track him down."

"I have to go to her." Jake pushed past his father and leaned over Tommy's bed. Brushing back his son's hair, he pressed a kiss to his forehead. "Gran and Gramps are going to stay with you for a bit, Tommy. But I'll be back soon. I promise."

Tommy didn't stir, compounding the weight in Jake's chest as he straightened. "I'll have my cell phone on me. Call me if anything changes."

Mom pulled Jake into a warm hug. "He'll be fine. And we'll be praying." She pushed him away. "Now go."

The midday traffic made the trip take twice as long as it should have. That and the police barricades stopping every car heading toward Hadyn. He didn't know whether to feel reassured that they were pulling out all the stops to catch this guy or terrified that they felt they needed to.

He pulled into the first available spot in the hospital's parking lot and raced toward the door.

"Hey," an older gentleman called after him. "You forgot the parking meter."

Jake ignored him. They could give him a thousand-dollar ticket for all he cared. He wasn't wasting a second longer than necessary. He plowed through the front doors, and at the sight of the crowd waiting for the elevators, veered toward the stairwell.

As he burst onto the fourth floor, a security guard caught his arm. "Where do you think you're going?"

Jake fought his hold. "Let go of me. I'm Jake Steele. Here to see a friend."

The marshal peeked out a door down the hall, a cell phone pressed to his ear. "It's okay," he said to the guard. "He's with us."

The guard released him with a nod, and Jake supposed he should be grateful that the guard was taking Kara's protection so seriously. He hurried to the marshal still standing in the doorway. "Any word on the manhunt?"

"I'll let him know," the marshal said into his cell phone, then stepped into the hall. "Yeah, just got word that they caught the guy. He had the child with him."

The tension leached from Jake's body. "Thank God."

"He said he'd been so desperate to adopt a child to reverse his wife's emotional collapse after their baby's stillbirth that he hadn't asked too many questions of the adoption agency. Of course, he's swearing up and down that he didn't hire any sniper. Claims he has no idea what the police are talking about. But Sam says he's a terrible liar."

Jake chuckled. "Sam would know."

A nurse carrying a tray of meds nodded to them and slipped into Kara's room.

"So does this mean Kara will be free to go home now?" *Or to stay?* Jake's pulse quickened at the thought of asking her.

"Soon. The feds will want to make sure we haven't missed anything."

"Hey." A nurse stepped out of a room down the hall and motioned to the security guard. "Did you see where my tray of meds went?"

"Kara!" Jake rammed past the marshal into Kara's room and tore back the curtain around her bed.

Her legs were kicking under the sheets as the woman smothered her face with a pillow. He grabbed the woman by the shoulders and flung her away from the bed just as Kara's legs stilled.

SIXTEEN

Terror gripped Jake's chest as he puffed another breath into Kara's mouth. "Breathe," he ordered, tilting his head to watch her chest rise and fall. He drew in another breath, expelled it into Kara's lungs. *Lord, please don't let her die.*

A team of doctors and nurses rushed into the room with a crash cart and pulled him away.

He crushed his fist to the pain tearing through his chest as he helplessly looked on. He'd never wanted to be in this place again. Losing one woman had been almost more than he could bear. Only…these past few nights, it hadn't been his wife that his arms had been aching to hold.

The marshal muscled the handcuffed "nurse" to the door with a white-knuckled grip.

Jake stopped him, straining to keep his fisted hands at his side. "Did you hire the sniper?"

"She should've minded her own business," the woman hissed, looking through him with cold, soulless eyes. "I saw her snapping pictures on that cell phone of hers."

So the husband had been chasing down his psychotic wife?

"Did your husband know you hired the sniper?"

She lifted her chin with an indignant sniff. "My husband would've let them take our baby away."

"Jake?"

Jake spun toward the sound of Kara's sweet voice, his heart soaring. The doctor and nurses stepped back and he rushed to her side. "Hey, how are you feeling?" He clasped her hands.

"You saved me."

He winked. "Any excuse to kiss a pretty woman works for me."

A rosy blush restored the color to her cheeks as her gaze dipped to his lips, then flicked to the nurses still crowding the room. "Is Tommy all better?"

Reflexively, his grasp tightened, and he had to force his fingers to relax again. "My parents are with him."

She searched his eyes as if she sensed what he wasn't saying.

"The woman who attacked you is the one you saw in the car in Boston," he said, not wanting to upset her by getting into Tommy's condition. "She and her husband are in custody. You're safe now."

She nodded, too many emotions to decipher swirling in her watery gaze. "Thanks to you."

"I told you I'd keep you safe. Remember? And now that you are, there's something I need to ask—"

A nurse burst into the room. "Are you Jake Steele?"

His heart lurched. "Yes. What is it?"

"There's an urgent phone call for you at the nurse's station. It's about Tom—"

Jake sprang toward the door.

"Jake?" Kara called after him. "Is Tommy okay?"

He paused at the door, digging his fingers into the frame to steel himself against the fears clamoring at his chest. "I don't know."

Clutching Rusty's leash, Kara paused in the deserted lobby of Seattle Children's Hospital. What would Jake say if he caught her here?

To think that little more than twenty-four hours ago, Jake had clung to her hand and looked at her as if he'd never let go. Now...he wasn't even returning her calls. Not that she blamed him after learning how emotionally traumatized Tommy was from the kidnapping. Sherri had tried to sugarcoat Jake's silence by saying that he'd probably been putting off calling until he had better news to share. But as true as his wanting to spare her might be, he had to resent her for Tommy's condition. How could he not?

Except even if Jake couldn't bear to face her, now that the marshal's office had given her the green light to return home, she couldn't leave without seeing Tommy. The last thing she wanted to do was cause Jake more pain. She owed him her life. But she had to at least try to help his son escape the dark world he'd sunk into.

Sherri motioned for Kara to follow her.

Kara's grip on the leash tightened as she sneaked Rusty onto the hospital elevator behind Sherri. "Are you sure this will be okay?"

"Yes, I already told you that the night nurse is a family friend. When I told her your idea of bringing Rusty to try to perk Tommy up, she thought it was fabulous. If he was an official therapy dog, we wouldn't even have to sneak him in."

"Yeah, but visiting hours ended two hours ago. If a security guard catches—" She darted glances to the top corners of the elevator. Whew, no cameras. She breathed normally again.

Sherri tapped the number for Tommy's floor and gave Kara a wink. "Don't worry. I asked my paramedic friend to preoccupy the security guard for a bit…if you know what I mean."

Kara forced a smile. She knew Sherri was trying to lighten the mood, but Kara was having a hard time finding anything amusing these days.

Not like her last night with Jake at the cabin when they'd laughed until they'd cried over that silly game of Pictionary. She sighed, and Rusty leaned his body against her leg in silent comfort.

Too soon, the elevator door slid open. An older woman smiled at them from the nurses' station. "You're right on time." She led the way to the end of the hall.

The *click-click* of Rusty's toenails on the tile floor echoed off the walls loud enough to wake every child on the ward. "You're sure Jake's not here?" Kara whispered to Sherri. "Because I don't think he'd be too happy about my bringing Rusty."

"You'd be surprised."

She gasped. "What? You promised me he wouldn't have to know. I can't—" The words lodged in her throat. As much as she wanted to see him, had hoped he'd call, she refused to put him on the spot. After the near smothering in her hospital room, she hadn't missed the way he'd joked about "any excuse to kiss a pretty woman" to gently dissuade her from thinking he had feelings for her. He was so sweet and kind that he'd probably do or say anything to make her feel better, as he had the first time she'd asked after Tommy. If not for the phone call that had sent him running from her hospital room, she still might not have known that Tommy had scarcely talked, let alone shown any interest in eating or playing, since the kidnapping. At least, his apparent turn for the worse had been short-lived, if Sherri could be believed.

Sherri hooked her arm through Kara's and tugged her forward. "C'mon. I'll make sure Jake's not there. What I meant was that he has a new appreciation for Rusty. After all, he did find his boy."

A smile tugged at Kara's lips, despite the churning in her stomach. She reached down and scratched behind Rusty's ears. "How could anyone not love this face?"

The nurse stopped in front of a door, and Kara's insides grew downright choppy. She drew in a deep breath as Sherri spoke quietly with the nurse. Her friend nodded and then entered the room as Sherri motioned Kara to wait. The swish of a curtain being drawn sounded, and a moment later the nurse returned smiling. "All set. Tommy's in the first bed."

The nightlight was on and Kara could just see his muss of downy blond hair above the blanket. Her throat knotted. He looked so tiny and alone, curled under the blankets, that she scarcely checked the urge to scoop him into her arms. Rusty must've felt the same because he started to whine.

"Shh," she chastised, and brought him to Tommy's bedside. Not wanting to frighten Tommy, she gently rubbed his arm and whispered, "Tommy, it's Kara. I brought someone to see you."

She heard Sherri rustling on the other side of the room, but kept her focus on Tommy. His hand poked out from beneath the blanket, and Rusty gave it a sloppy kiss.

Tommy's eyes popped open. She hunched down so he could see her. He rubbed his eyes. "Kara?"

She smiled. "Hi, sport. I've missed you. How you doing?"

His head shifted sideways on the pillow, and one shoulder lifted in a shrug. Rusty gave Tommy's hand another wash and Tommy's eyes widened.

Kara chuckled. "Someone else missed you, too. Mind if he snuggles up there with you for a while?"

Tommy scooted his body back to make room. "You sure it's okay?" he whispered conspiratorially.

"Nope." Kara grinned. "But I won't tell if you won't." She patted the bed. "Rusty, up."

The dog didn't need to be told twice. He jumped up and gave Tommy's face a thorough lick. Tommy's laughter between sputters was music to Kara's ears. She threw a grin to Sherri over her shoulder, but...

Jake, not Sherri, stood at the edge of the curtain, his expression unreadable in the shadows.

The knot in Kara's throat thickened. "I'm sorry. I know I probably should've asked you if it was okay. But I wasn't sure you'd agree. And I so wanted to help Tommy. I knew that—"

He stepped around the bed, the ravages of too many sleepless nights bruising his handsome face. Her breath bottled in her lungs as he closed the distance between them, his expression intense.

Unable to get another word past the constriction in her throat, all she could do was stare at the emotions battling for dominance on his face.

He lifted his hand to her cheek with a reverence that stole her breath. "You came," he whispered, his gaze hungrily raking over her face as his lips stretched into a jubilant smile.

"I would have come soon—"

He swept her into his arms and swallowed the rest of her excuses in a world-tilting kiss. A kiss that reached into her heart and shattered all the barricades that had vigilantly guarded it for as long as she could remember. Pulling back from the kiss, he cradled her face and touched his forehead to hers. "I tried calling your hospital room this morning and they said you'd gone."

He'd called. Kara's heart scrambled to find its footing. But Jake's eyes shone with a love so tangible her heart didn't stand a chance. Joy as she'd never known exploded in her chest. She drew his mouth back to hers and poured all her love for this man and his little boy, her gratitude for his protectiveness, her admiration of his solid faith, her hopes that he'd ask her to stay, into kissing him back.

Beside them, Tommy giggled. And this time, she sensed it wasn't thanks to the dog's exuberant kisses. She and Jake opened their eyes, their lips still touching, and smiled as together they turned to look at Tommy. As if they could read each other's minds, they grinned at each other again and then jumped on the bed to kiss Tommy. The dog got in a few more swipes of his own, and they were soon a giggling mass of people and dog.

The overhead light clicked on. Sherri and the nurse stood in the doorway, grinning. "I told you it would work," she said smugly, except Kara had the niggling suspicion she wasn't talking about the dog cheering up Tommy. The nurse chuckled and, steering Sherri back into the hall, closed the door.

Jake and Kara leaned against the pillows on the narrow hospital bed with Tommy and Rusty nestled between them. "Now that you're better, you gonna come back and stay at Gran and Gramps's?" he asked. "Daddy said they caught the bad man so you don't have to stay in the cabin anymore."

Caught the bad woman, too, thanks to his daddy. Of course, the deputy marshal said their defense lawyers were already angling for an insanity plea, and the wealthy pair wouldn't have any trouble making bail, but at least the baby had finally been safely returned to his desperate parents. And yeah, Kara was free to live wherever she wanted. She smiled at Tommy, her heart bursting with the yearning to say yes to living here. But she needed more than the invitation of a five-year-old boy to do that. And suddenly she couldn't lift her gaze past Jake's chest. Her heart raced. What if all this had been joy over Tommy's awakening, not…?

Jake shifted sideways, and reaching over Tommy's head, cupped Kara's jaw in his warm hands. The pad of his thumb traced her bottom lip. "I have a better idea."

Her heart jittered as she slowly lifted her gaze from his chest, to his chin, his lips, his nose and finally rested on his pure blue eyes brimming with love and yearning and…maybe a little uncertainty. "I love you, Kara. From the moment you turned into my arms to escape that reporter's camera, I haven't been able to stop thinking about you, wanting to protect you, wanting to be with you. You've awakened in me something I didn't think I'd ever feel again. And Tommy adores you."

"Rusty, too," Tommy chirped up.

"There you go," Jake said, as if that clinched everything. He grinned, the corners of his eyes crunching in the most heart-skipping way. "I know your home and family and teaching job are in Boston, and—"

"But Uncle Sam says Stalwart's way better than Boston. He just moved back. Tell her," Tommy said.

As if muffling a chuckle, Jake's chest shuddered. "As I was saying, for the past few days, I've been trying to convince myself that it wasn't fair to ask you to stay."

Kara's heart swelled with anticipation. "Could you just spit out what you want to say, firefighter? Because if you keep me in suspense much longer, my heart might burst."

"I'm good at AR—mouth-to-mouth." He winked. Then, holding her gaze, he offered a brief, tantalizingly sweet demonstration.

"Mmm, you might be handy to keep around. You know? For emergencies."

Tommy pulled on his shirtsleeve. "What's your better idea, Daddy?"

Jake's lip quivered as if he was suddenly nervous that she might not give him the answer that she suspected—hoped—he was fishing for.

She opened her mouth to reassure him that

she shared his feelings, but he pressed a finger to her lips.

"Kara, Nicole, Connie Klumchuck—" his eyes twinkled "—or whatever you want me to call you, I have fallen utterly and completely in love with you. I want you in my life, my son's life, not just as my parents' houseguest." He shot his son a lame-idea look and then slid his hands down her neck, gingerly past her wounded shoulder to her hands, which he clasped to his chest. "Would you do me the honor of becoming my wife?"

Tears spilled down her cheeks, and she couldn't stop her lips from quivering.

"I promise I'll take you to visit Boston as often as you want," Jake quickly added.

Kara laughed through her happy tears and, pulling her hands from his grasp, threw her arms around his neck. "Yes! Nothing would make me happier than being your wife."

"Mine, too!" Tommy chimed in, hugging her waist.

Jake wrapped his arms around all of them. "She'll be your mother, Tommy. How's that sound?"

"Cool!" Tommy cried.

"Wonderful," Kara agreed.

Rusty woofed his agreement, too.

"Yes, I see what you mean," a deep male voice said from the doorway. A man wearing a lab coat, a stethoscope curled around his neck, stood beside Sherri's nurse friend. He strode to the bed, fixing his stethoscope into his ears.

Sherri appeared at the door after him, pale and mouthing apologies as Kara scooted off the bed, dragging Rusty with her.

Jake slid out the other side of the bed as the doctor listened to Tommy's chest, took his pulse, looked at his eyes. "Yes," he repeated. "Hospitals are for sick people, young man." He made a notation on his clipboard, then handed it to the nurse. "I'm afraid you don't qualify. It's time you went home." He cleared his throat. "And don't forget to take your dog and new mom with you." He winked at Kara as he turned on his heel and strode out.

Sherri rushed forward and gave Kara a big hug. "Let me be the first to welcome you to the family."

Easing the dog leash from Kara's hand, Jake tapped Sherri on the shoulder, then handed her the leash. "How about you help Tommy get dressed and call to let my mom and dad know we'll soon be on our way home, while I show Kara a real family welcome?"

As Sherri scurried out of his way, Jake slipped into her place and, tangling his fingers in her hair once again, said, "Now, where were we?"

A smile so wide overtook her that she could

feel it spread through her chest. "I believe that I had just said yes." With supreme effort, she reined in her smile and proffered a serious tone. "But I'm afraid that I may have neglected to say something very important."

His fingers teasing the tiny hairs at the nape of her neck stilled. "Oh?"

She hid a smile at the nervousness in his voice. "Yes, Mr. Jake Steele. Steele is my preferred last name, by the way."

"Duly noted," he said with mock seriousness. "Is that what you neglected to tell me?"

Her smile broke loose. "No…I think I might have neglected to mention that you are the bravest, most caring, tenderhearted, stubbornly protective man I have ever met, and the second happiest day of my life was the day you chased me down."

"Only the second happiest?"

She moistened her lips. "Today is the happiest. I love you with all of my heart."

He crushed her to his chest, capturing her lips in a possessive kiss that held nothing back. Sherri cleared her throat, reminding them of their audience, and he relaxed his embrace with an unapologetic grin. "How do you feel about a Christmas wedding?"

EPILOGUE

Jake turned his truck onto his street and glanced across the seat at his future in-laws. They looked as nervous as he felt, and this time the fluttery sensation in his stomach wasn't the euphoria he hoped he never stopped feeling whenever he was about to see his bride-to-be.

No, today the gymnastics in his stomach had nothing to do with anticipation.

Flying in his bride-to-be's estranged parents suddenly did not feel like the kind of surprise he should spring on Kara without warning.

"It sounds as if you have a fine family, Jake. And I can tell by the way you talk about our daughter that you love her very much." Mr. Redman reached for his wife's hand and twined his fingers through hers, a testament to their enduring affection that he hoped could only bode well for their upcoming reunion with Kara.

"Nicole always wanted lots of cousins and

aunts and uncles and siblings," Mrs. Redman added wistfully.

Jake chuckled. "Yeah, she's mentioned that a few times." He still didn't understand why Kara—the name she'd decided to keep since it was as Kara that she'd found her forever love—hadn't jumped at the green light to call her parents the second the deputy marshal had officially released her from witness security. He'd worried that she was afraid they'd make a big stink about her staying in Washington State instead of returning to Boston, and that she didn't want to spoil their first Christmas together, and possibly the wedding.

But her parents didn't act as if they'd make a fuss. And despite Kara's dismissal of his offer to put off the wedding so that her friends and family might have more time to make plans to join them, or even to have the wedding in Boston, he'd sensed yearning rippling beneath her no.

As they rounded the bend, Mrs. Redman gasped and pointed to the windshield. "There she is."

Kara and Tommy were hanging spruce garland and Christmas lights along the porch rails. Her eyes had gleamed when she'd asked him if he'd mind her decorating his house for the holidays. Growing up in an apartment, she'd always dreamed of having a real tree and decorating outdoors and having a big Christmas dinner, she'd said, and he was looking forward to taking her and Tommy on her first tree-hunting expedition tomorrow.

Rusty pinched a velvet bow from the garland and a mad chase ensued, ending in a three-way tug-of-war with Kara's hair tangling around her face, laughter filling the air.

"I've never seen her happier," Mr. Redman said, his voice cracking.

His heart hammering, Jake prayed he could say the same a few minutes from now. He flicked on his signal for the driveway and Kara whirled toward the truck. Her arm froze midwave, her gaze connecting with her parents. Her jaw dropped open.

Jake parked across from where she continued to stand like a gorgeous Greek statue, minus that gaping mouth. Tommy raced to the passenger side of the truck and yanked open the door, Rusty yipping at his heels. "Hi, I'm Tommy," he said as Jake rounded the truck, needing to close the distance between Kara and him before she recovered from the shock.

Mrs. Redman hopped from the truck and hunkered down in front of Tommy. "Well, hello, Tommy. I'm Mrs. Redman...."

Jake clasped Kara's hands and dipped his head to capture her gaze. It remained fixed on her mother, now caught in a neck hug with his son, who was enthusiastically telling the world he'd always wanted another grandmother. "Am I in the doghouse?"

Kara blinked and looked at him. "You called my parents," she whispered.

He thumbed the diamond solitaire glittering on her finger and gave her a sheepish look. "I didn't feel right marrying you among all my family and friends and not at least making the effort. You may be all grown-up, but you're still their little girl. Trust me, no parent wants to miss such an important day in their child's life. I feel terrible if I have to miss one of the events at Tommy's kids' club."

She snorted. "My parents didn't share your sentiment." Her gaze strayed to her father, who was edging his way across the truck seat toward the door, looking a lot older and warier than he had a few minutes ago. She turned her back to the truck. "At least not my dad. He never even made it to my high school graduation ceremony."

"I heard," Jake said.

"You did?"

"I was telling him on the drive from the airport," her dad said from behind her. "I felt terrible about missing it. I even rented a car to try to get home in time when my flight got diverted because of the storm."

Kate spun on her heel to face him. "The weather was perfect on my graduation day."

"Not the day before," her father said softly.

"You left a day early? Really?"

Jake brushed his knuckles across her cheek. "He said he tried to explain, but you wouldn't talk to him."

"I thought he was just making excuses."

Her dad shook his head. "Not that time. But I can't blame you for thinking as much. I missed far too many important days in your life. And I'm sorry for that." He reached for her hands. "But I was determined not to miss *this* one. The instant I got off the phone with Jake, I booked the first flight I could get."

She stared at him, looking dumbfounded. "But you didn't seem to care when I told you that I needed to be out of contact for a while."

"Didn't care?" Disbelief pitched his voice higher. "I've been on the phone with the police every day for the past three months, getting assurances you were still alive. Don't you know how much I love you?"

Kara threw her arms around her father's neck. "Oh, Daddy, I'm so glad you're here."

Her father pulled back, his hands still on her shoulders, and looked at her with tears in his eyes. "Me, too, sweetie. Me, too."

Jake sidled closer and gave her a sideways hug. "So you like your surprise?"

Giving him a wink, her father stepped back. "Excuse me. I need to meet my grandson."

Kara soared into Jake's arms. "Thank you!" She tipped her head back and gave him a teasingly scolding look. "Not that I want you to make a habit of not listening to me, you understand, but—" she pressed a palm to her mouth "—I was afraid they wouldn't want to come. I figured it would hurt less not to ask than to have them not show up."

"Oh, babe…" He pulled her close and kissed her sweet lips. "There's no place they'd rather be." He traced her moistened lips with the pad of his thumb, his heart beating wildly. "But I should warn you to enjoy their visit now—" he kissed the tip of her nose and quirked his lips mischievously "—because after our wedding, I'm not sharing you with anyone for at least a week." He tugged her closer. She smelled like Christmas trees and fresh air and…cinnamon. "Mmm. Maybe two weeks. I like to take my time unwrapping my Christmas presents."

A becoming blush rosied her cheeks. "I don't know…. Tommy might not be so easily won over to the idea of a *two*-week honeymoon. You've already agreed to let him keep the dog at our house. What will be next? A cat?"

"Hmm." He nibbled her bottom lip. "How about a baby brother or sister?"

Her joyous laughter filled the recesses of his soul.

Hugging her close, he twirled her in a circle. "You are the best Christmas gift I could ever have hoped for."

* * * * *

Dear Reader,

We daily face moral choices in the little things we choose to do or say, or not do or say, and probably spend little time contemplating the consequences beforehand. Although when we do, we tend to make choices that limit our own discomfort, don't we?

Despite her boyfriend's warning, Kara couldn't have imagined the dire situation she'd face by reporting what she saw in the park. Yet even in the midst of her troubles, Kara knows she couldn't have lived with herself if she'd made a different choice. Jake faces similar crossroads throughout the story—times when he could choose to back away from helping Kara for his family's safety, a noble reason. Yet, he doesn't.

How about you? Has Kara and Jake's story inspired you to make a hard decision in your own life and trust God for the outcome? I'd love to hear about it and pray for you. You can reach me via email at sandraorchard@ymail.com, or at www.facebook.com/SandraOrchard.

I'm superexcited to share paramedic Sherri Steele's story in the new year. To learn more about that and explore fun bonus features for all of my novels, please visit me online at www.sandraorchard.com and sign up for my newsletter for exclusive subscriber giveaways—including more Christmas stories!

Sincerely,
Sandra Orchard

Questions for Discussion

1. In Kara's experience, beginning with her father, men can't be counted on to be there when needed. How a person relates to his or her father can have a huge impact on how he or she sees God. How have your childhood experiences affected your perception of God?

2. Jake felt as if he let his wife down in failing to prevent her death. Have you (or someone you cared about) ever lost a spouse, or suffered under such grief that you mistakenly blamed yourself as Jake did in regards to his wife's death?

3. Have you ever felt a strong moral responsibility similar to Kara's over reporting what she witnessed in the park? Have you ever had a well-meaning friend try to talk you out of it? What did you do?

4. Where or to whom do you turn to find the courage to do what is right?

5. Kara always yearned to share with her parents more of the traditions that accompany holiday celebrations, such as decorating

and sharing meals with extended family or friends. What does a perfect holiday celebration look like for you?

6. The deputy marshal handling Kara's witness protection warned her to never tell anyone who she really is and to not trust anyone, because the person could be luring her into a false sense of security. Have you ever trusted someone you shouldn't have? What happened?

7. How do you decide if someone can be trusted? What precautions do you take to guard against your trust being used against you?

8. At the outset of the story, Jake has a low opinion of the dog his parents adopted for his son. Have you ever had a pet or known a pet that turned out to give back so much more than you had imagined?

9. Jake's parents took Kara into their home without hesitation and offered her a room to stay as long as she needed it. Does that kind of hospitality come naturally to you, or do you find it difficult to open your home to outsiders? Why do you think that is?

10. Since losing his wife, his son was Jake's world. Yet experts warn married couples against putting their children (aside from basic needs) ahead of their spouse. What do you think?

LARGER-PRINT BOOKS!

GET 2 FREE LARGER-PRINT NOVELS PLUS 2 FREE MYSTERY GIFTS

Love Inspired

Larger-print novels are now available...